SIREN SONG

JJ MARSH

PREWETT
BIELMANN

Published by Prewett Bielmann Ltd.
All enquiries to admin@jjmarshauthor.com

First printing, 2023
eBook Edition:
ISBN 978-3-906256-21-4

Paperback:
ISBN 978-3-906256-22-1

1

Adrian possessed many wonderful characteristics but at that precise moment the one Beatrice loved most was his willingness to dawdle. Wander around a museum, stop for a sit-down and refreshments. Queue for the Sagreda Familia, have a rest in Parc Güell. Watch Will tearing along a beach in 25° heat while sitting in the shade with an ice-cream. Beatrice needed frequent stops because thrilling as Barcelona was, it was also hectic, crowded with tourists and not yet Easter, but exhaustingly hot.

The Surrealists had the most extraordinary imaginations. Buildings resembling loaves of bread or melting honeycombs stood on street corners as if they were nothing special. Tiled paths and riotous sculpture filled the parks and colour burst from every doorway and window. At the same time, traffic clogged the streets and wave after wave of sightseers billowed around every monument. With pungent markets, the clatter of pigeons and competing musical tastes of streetside cafés, Barcelona overloaded every sense.

Will, Adrian and Beatrice had been in the capital of Catalonia for five days, gearing up for the main event. On Thursday, Will would take part in the Iron Man competition: swimming, cycling and running a marathon alongside thousands of other contestants. Although Beatrice couldn't understand the attraction of haring around like a mad thing in such conditions, she did admire his stamina. She and Adrian found a spot at the end of the swim and the start of the cycle race, watching from a covered marquee. They drank iced coffee, applauded occasionally and tried to spot Will among the crowds of emerging competitors. Once Adrian thought he saw him until Beatrice pointed out Will was wearing a red T-shirt, not white. Eventually they got bored and wandered off to do some souvenir shopping. La Boqueria Market looked like a good place to order some lunch. Filled with punchy colours and pungent scents, it was enough to knock a person off her feet.

When faced with a plethora of choices of cafés and restaurants displaying the most appetising dishes, Beatrice was stymied. Adrian talked her into a little place on the corner with colourful tiles and a house paella. When it came in a huge copper platter, with rice the colour of saffron surrounding all manner of seafood, Beatrice was very glad she had given in.

"Oh, wow, that looks absolutely delicious!" Adrian exclaimed.

The young waitress gave him an appreciative smile. "Best paella in Barcelona! Don't take my word for it, look at the tourist guide. Enjoy your meal."

"Thank you. We certainly will," said Adrian, topping up Beatrice's wine. "Didn't I tell you I have an instinct for these sorts of things? Plus the fact this place has tables and comfy chairs unlike one of those authentic but uncomfortable counters. Dig in."

Beatrice scooped two spoonfuls onto her plate, making sure she included cockles, prawns and mussels. "You did and you are right. This is infinitely preferable to perching on a stool at a counter. To tell you the truth, my feet have had more than enough tramping city streets this week. I'm very much looking forward to our sojourn at the beach."

"You're not the only one. I know I always claim to be a city boy at heart, but when I'm on holiday, I feel I deserve greenery, beaches, countryside and all that jazz. Maybe it's because of what happened on Monday, but I don't feel a hundred percent able to relax."

Beatrice gave a commiserating nod. It was most unfortunate Adrian had been robbed on the first day of their arrival. Will had given them a stern lecture on not allowing themselves to get distracted and how to keep their valuables safe. They made it through the airport, into a taxi and arrived at their apartment without mishap, congratulating themselves on being street savvy. Then Adrian popped along the street to buy a few provisions and was accosted by a young woman crying for help. While he attempted to ascertain the nature of the problem, someone lifted his wallet.

Therefore, his first few hours in their holiday apartment were not spent sipping Cava on the balcony but on the phone to the bank cancelling cards and visiting the police station to report a theft. Thankfully, Adrian had taken Will's advice and kept his phone and contactless debit card separate from the other items in his wallet, so only lost €250, his credit card, a London transport travel card and a handwritten list of recommendations from his Catalonian ex-boyfriend.

"I can understand how you feel. It was a rotten thing to happen. I must say, you handled it very well. Some people would allow such an incident to ruin the entire holiday, but you took it in your stride. Isn't this paella extraordinary? I don't think I've ever eaten something as unctuous."

Adrian nodded with some enthusiasm. "It's divine. Thank you for saying that. It's one of the things I've been working on with my therapist, you know, not blowing a minor inconvenience out of proportion. She says it will help me not only in my daily life, but when Will and I come to relocate. It's a question of adaptation if you think about it. Someone picking my pocket is not the end of the world and I have learned a lesson. When we do move to Amsterdam, I'm going to encounter lots of new experiences and not all of them will be pleasant. With the right mindset, I can see them for what they are, chalking each one up to an education. If I don't, I'm likely to spend the first few months sulking and resentful of my new environment. Anyway, if Dolly can cope with a new country, so can Adrian Harvey. Would you pass the bread?"

"Here. Of course you can cope. As for Dolly, she'll be at home wherever you are. Dogs are very adaptable, especially when young. How's the Dutch going?"

Adrian tore into a bread roll. "Very well indeed! I'm a natural, according to my teacher. I think it's partly to do with my musicality and ear for accents but I'm picking it up far more quickly than I ever did with German. How's your French course?"

"Your motivation is different this time. You only made a half-hearted stab at learning German because you were madly in love with Holger. That didn't last and neither did your passion for the language. Dutch is the language of your new home, so you're bound to feel a greater affinity. My French course is stimulating a lot of passive knowledge I didn't know I had. It's been donkeys' ears since I last spoke it. Best of all, it's a lovely way to meet people."

"That's true. You have no choice but to be sociable with your fellow students. What do they do with this rice? I'd love to get the recipe and try it at home, wherever that will be." His phone buzzed and he glanced at the screen with a smile. "It's Jared. He just sent me his list of must-sees again after that bastard nicked my wallet. Not only is this very market on the list, but he recommends eating paella in one of the corner restaurants. I have a nose, I tell you." He started composing a reply.

"Sweet man. Send him my love." She helped herself to another spoonful, even though her stomach was satiated. "For a second there, I thought it might be Will, finishing early."

Adrian snorted. "If he finished this early, he'd be Superman, not Iron Man. The course takes the average triathlete at least twelve hours. He won't be done till at least dinner time and then he'll collapse into bed. As mid-life crises go, I suppose it could be worse. So we have an afternoon free to do exactly as we please. Shall we have a look at Jared's list or do you have a burning desire to see a particular work of art?"

A family group entered the restaurant and settled themselves at a nearby table, two adults with four children ranging in age from teens to toddlers. Each of them sat down and studied the menu.

"Everyone takes eating quite seriously here," Beatrice observed. "I approve. You know, there's one Spanish tradition I've not yet tried." She placed her knife and fork together on her plate.

Adrian gave her a knowing smile. "Somehow I doubt it's flamenco dancing. Would you like to head back to the flat and have a siesta?"

"You read my mind. Unless that scuppers your plans?"

"My plans extend to lounging on the sofa and editing my photos for Instagram. Why shouldn't we spend a couple of hours appreciating the comforts of our apartment while Action Man is occupied? Without him urging us onto the next stop of our itinerary, we can revert to old habits. I'll get the bill."

. . .

Three hours later, Beatrice awoke in her bedroom, refreshed and relaxed. Some might say she was showing her age by needing an afternoon nap. Her retort would be 'When in Spain ...'.

In any case, the rest had done her good. She loved Adrian and Will like family members, but it was hard to spend two weeks in anyone's company without needing a little me-time. She slipped on a loose linen dress and wandered into the living-room to find Adrian. He was not, as she expected, supine on the settee. His shoes were by the door, his wine glass empty and his bedroom door was closed. Another one had succumbed. She poured herself a beaker of water, sat on the balcony and watched the world go by. Upton St Nicholas it was not. The chaos and volume of the street below drove her indoors after five minutes. The Iron Man contest should be coming to a close shortly. She switched on the television, muted the volume and tried to make sense of the mass of bodies running towards the camera.

Poor things, they looked fit to drop. Gritted teeth, limbs slick with sweat, some weaving as if their internal compass had gone awry and others pounding the final kilometre as if no other objective existed; the whole thing was a bizarre exercise in Beatrice's view. She watched for fifteen minutes, hoping to spot Will's red shirt but the runners became a blur and her thoughts turned to dinner.

"Guess what?"

Adrian's voice startled her into a gasp.

"Sorry, sorry, I thought you were watching telly. But guess what?"

"I have no idea. What is it?"

Adrian flopped onto the sofa beside her, carrying his laptop. He smelt of thyme and lemons, like a Tuscan breeze. "Well, I was thinking. After the Iron Man excesses, Will is going to be exhausted. You and I did all the museums, markets and sights, so we're ready for some relaxing vibes, right? This is our holiday, let's not forget. So Mister Sophistication here just contacted our accommodation in Sitges and switched the dates. We can move in tomorrow!"

A surge of delight overcame Beatrice but her natural caution raised objections. "How marvellous! You don't think Will might mind?"

"As I said, he will be pretty much comatose this evening and open to all suggestions. I'll spin this as a special award for all his efforts and then we bundle him onto a train in the morning. *Fait accompli*! We have a cosy little place near the beach and Sitges is too cute. Winding little alleyways, shops full of trinkets and gay as the day is long. You will love it!" He tilted his screen in her direction.

It looked idyllic. No traffic, blue shutters, cobbled streets, white walls and shady corners with a view of the ocean.

"Let's do it! Should we try and meet Will at the finish line or in that bar?"

The finish line was a hopeless case, crammed with reporters, TV crews, supporters, families and the usual gawkers. Adrian guided Beatrice to a wine bar on a street corner and ordered them both a glass of Rioja. They sat outside on stumpy stools around a barrel, scanning the streets for any sign of the Iron Man.

"This is the right place, I'm one hundred percent convinced. I even took a card to remind me. He'll shower in the communal bathroom, meet us here for a drink and celebrate his triumph. Whether he'll be able to eat or speak remains to be seen. It's been almost thirteen hours, Beatrice, I'm starting to worry. The worst thing is that I cannot call him. He leaves his phone behind. Weight, water, you know." Adrian waggled a hand as if fanning himself.

"Calm down. You know your husband. He's a planner. He trained his body and his mind, studied the route, worked out exactly how to find us and if I know Will, chose the perfect champagne to toast his triumph. He will get here when he's ready. Please stop jiggling your leg because this barrel is not the most stable." She looked up and saw Adrian's attention was elsewhere.

"Will!" He jumped up and opened his arms. "My hero!"

A taxi had pulled up alongside the pavement. Will eased himself from the back seat, evidently in pain. On seeing his husband, he broke into a relieved smile. Adrian rushed to embrace him, all tenderness and joy. Their absorption in one another gave Beatrice a moment to see a young Spanish man exit the cab and pay the driver. He came to stand awkwardly on the kerb near Will.

"I'm fine, I'm fine. It was tough, in this heat, but I made it. Look!" He withdrew a certificate from his pocket. "Lady and gentleman, you are looking at a bona fide Iron Man. Beatrice, Adrian, let me introduce you to my friend, Manu. Without him, I couldn't have earned this. Manu, this is my husband, Adrian, and our best friend, Beatrice."

Beatrice got to her feet and filled the gap left by Adrian's puzzlement. "Hello, Manu. I'm pleased to meet you. Are you also an Iron Man?"

If Beatrice had still been operating as a detective inspector with the Metropolitan Police, she would instantly have suspected Manu of being a drug user. His reactions were slow and his eyes are bloodshot. Then again he had been swimming, cycling and running for longer than Beatrice had been awake.

"Beatriz is the name of my sister. Yes, I am an Iron Man. Can I sit down?"

"Let's all sit down before my knees give way," said Will.

Adrian dragged over two more stools and beckoned the waitress. "Champagne all round?" he asked.

Manu shook his head. "Not champagne, sorry." He spoke to the waitress in what Beatrice assumed must be Catalan, as she recognised very few words.

He turned back to them. "We drink Corpinnat. And water." He was a short, squat man with a thick moustache, heavy brows and a ready grin which he flashed at Will.

"Oh, yeah, we need plenty of water. Let me explain." Will brushed a hand over his damp hair and rested his hand on Adrian's leg. "The swimming was fine and I finished early. The cycling was challenging but nothing worse than expected. Then I set off on the marathon. Twenty kilometres in, I was into my groove until I hit a wall. I lost it completely, started staggering and looked for a steward so I could give up and get some help. That's when Manu slowed to walk beside me, cupped his arm under my elbow and handed me a bottle of water. He made me keep going, just stumbling along the route but going in the right direction. When I found some deep reserves of energy, we ran again. Every time I flagged, Manu was right there, encouraging me to take another step. We crossed the line together and I know I couldn't have done it without him." He reached his hand high into the air and Manu clasped it.

She was a daft old sap, she knew that, but the naked gratitude between the two men filled Beatrice's eyes with tears. "What a wonderful story! Manu, thank you for being a good Samaritan. Ah! Here's the fizz."

The waitress poured four glasses of wheat-coloured bubbles and left two bottles of water on the barrel.

Adrian raised his glass. "Congratulations to Will and Manu! Quite the achievement! Well done, gentlemen."

They joined in the toast but Beatrice could see neither

sportsman had a taste for alcohol. She was about to leap into Small-Talk mode when Adrian made his announcement.

"In other news, I brought forward our rental in Sitges. We can move in tomorrow!"

"Tomorrow? We booked from Monday."

"I know. But Beatrice and I thought you deserved a reward after today, such as relaxing on the beach and regaining your strength. I've sorted everything out. We can leave in the morning."

Beatrice noted how she had been saddled with the change of plan and watched Will with a keen eye.

"I see. Right. I was kind of looking forward to a few days exploring the city now I've finished training. Not only that but Manu has invited us all for lunch on Saturday to meet his family. Weird you didn't consult me before changing our plans."

Tension buzzed across the table and Manu shifted in his seat. "It's no problem, Will. Sitges is half an hour away on the train. If you still want to come, you're welcome. You too, Beatrice. If you need help with anything during your stay, just give me a call. How do you like Barcelona?"

Beatrice set her elbows on the barrel and rested her chin on her knuckles. "Intense is probably the word I'd choose. As if I've been in fifth gear all week. It's a lot to take in. Have you lived here all your life?"

"No, I come from a small town north of Barcelona called Figueres."

"Oh, I've heard of that. Didn't Dalí live there?"

"He did. It's not far away and worth a visit."

"Good tip. How come you speak such fluent English?" She shot a glance at Will and Adrian who were having a row, *sotto voce.*

"In the art world, it's a must. I spent two years in London, training with Sotheby's. What do you think of the Corpinnat?"

"Quite delicious! Sotheby's, you said? Are you an art dealer?"

"Yes, but only as a hobby. By profession, I am an auctioneer."

"How fascinating! I've never met an auctioneer before."

Will forestalled any further discussion by accepting Manu's invitation to lunch on Saturday on behalf of all three of them. When the Spaniard rose to leave, Will heaved himself to his feet for a hearty embrace. Manu shared a business card and reiterated his offer of assistance, shaking everyone's hand twice. The poor man looked as if his legs might collapse at any moment and headed off towards the nearest Metro. Adrian excused himself and went in search of the bathroom.

"The move to Sitges wasn't your idea, was it?" asked Will, tipping the water into his empty flute.

"No, it wasn't. That said, I'm more than ready to get out of the city and sit by the seaside. Perhaps Adrian sensed my old-lady exhaustion and made an executive decision so that both of us could rest and in your case, recover."

Will raised an eyebrow. "Always the diplomat."

"Always the detective. You have a drive, Will, and I admire it enormously. Adrian and I are more of the pleasure-seeking sort, but I want you to know this. I am enormously proud of you for making a plan and sticking to it. You are more than an Iron Man because you have an iron will."

He squeezed her arm. "Thank you."

"So can we go to Sitges or not?"

He laughed, the tension leaving his brow. "Yeah, let's go to the beach. But first I want to eat a shitload of carbs and sleep for at least twelve hours."

Adrian appeared at Will's shoulder with a wary smile. "Peace?"

"Not unless I get a massive paella in the next thirty minutes." He drained his water and registered their guilty faces. "You've already had one. You pair of bastards!"

The journey to Sitges began with a grim view –
graffitied windows and industrial warehouses – but
lightened up when the train emerged onto the coastline. Beatrice and Adrian admired the views of the sea, gasped at
the proximity of hikers to the railway line and made no secret of
their holiday high spirits. Will gave the occasional indulgent
smile when he wasn't reading the news on his phone. The
second they disembarked onto the platform, Beatrice was
charmed.

Sitges reminded her of Santorini, a spectacularly pretty
Greek island she had once visited while trying to catch a serial
killer. Pretty houses, vibrant window boxes, winding streets and
a languid air reminiscent of Brighton endeared them all in the
first five minutes. Will found the apartment, accessed the keys
and within half an hour, they were reclining on their own little
balcony with a sea view.

"Perfect!" Adrian pronounced.

"Idyllic," Beatrice agreed.

"It's a handy spot," said Will. "Easy walk to the station,
every kind of restaurant within a stone's throw, Barcelona is

thirty minutes away and there are lots of hikes along the coast."

Beatrice snorted into her orange juice. "You're still limping after yesterday's exertions! How about a nice sit down for a couple of days? All I want to do is potter about, read in a deckchair and fall asleep whenever the opportunity arises. Adrian?"

"Likewise. Beatrice and I are soul mates. Apart from the gay thing, obviously. Shall we wander down to one of the beaches and have lunch on the seafront?"

"Yeah, let's explore the town today. But I warn you, I want to make the most of this week. We don't have to do everything together, but I plan to use every minute of my fortnight off."

Adrian mugged a fearful expression. "In that case, Iron Man, make us a G&T. One must always have an aperitif before lunch."

They spent the day at a leisurely pace, lingering over lunch, wandering around the fortifications, browsing tourist shops and sampling coffee in a beachside café. Normally an impatient fidget, Will was content to rest and relax in the spring sunshine while Adrian read interesting nuggets from the guidebook.

"I quite fancy this museum, Le Palais Maricel. It's just round the corner from that church we saw. Look, it's all ceramics, murals and sculptures and an architect's dream. Shall we go?"

Will pushed up his sunglasses to view the pictures. "Yeah, that looks special. Beatrice? What about you?"

"It does look quite lovely, I agree, but I'm a little over museum-ed at the moment. My plan is to sit here a little longer then drift back to the apartment for an afternoon nap. Sitges suits me down to the ground. Everything is relaxed and unthreatening. Plus I can't get lost."

"OK. We'll see you later. Stay out of trouble," said Adrian.

She watched them go with a sympathetic smile at Will's stiffness and Adrian's bounce then turned her attention to the sea.

There was something profoundly soothing about smelling the ozone, listening to the waves, while watching the gulls screech and wheel through the air. It was tempting to doze off, but the café was getting increasingly crowded and she was taking up space. She looked around for the waiter so she could pay the bill.

"Excuse me? Would you mind if I sat here?" An older woman in a paisley-print dress stood beside the chair recently vacated by Will.

"Not at all, I was just leaving." She moved the empty coffee cups out of the way.

"Thank you, you're very kind. One can see the season has started in earnest. Up until now I've had my choice of seats on the terrace. Not anymore."

"Oh, are you a local? Because you spoke English I assumed you were a tourist, like me."

The woman's face creased into a warm smile. "Yes, I live locally. After twenty years in Salisbury, I returned to the town of my birth. At my age, the weather makes all the difference."

The waiter came over and greeted the lady by name. They had brief chat and she gave her order. The waiter looked expectantly at Beatrice.

"Would you like to join me in my afternoon treat? It's a Spanish coffee, by which I mean coffee spiked with rum and Gran Marnier. One of those with a *buñuelo de viento* will see you through to dinner time."

Beatrice had no idea what a *buñuelo de viento* was but her curiosity was piqued. "That sounds fascinating. Yes please, I will join you as long as you allow me to pick up the tab."

The waiter nodded. "*Vale.* Afternoon tea for two." He returned inside the café.

"My name is Mia," said the lady, offering her hand.

Beatrice shook it. "I'm Beatrice. Pleased to meet you Mia. I've never heard of the Spanish coffee, at least the sort you describe. And what was the other thing?"

"*Buñuelo de viento*. A cross between a doughnut and a choux bun. They're very light. *Viento* means wind. If you have a sweet tooth, you will love them." She reached behind her head and released her hair clip. A skein of grey hair tumbled over her shoulders. "Oh, that's better. I have to wear my hair up when I'm working so it's a relief to let it loose."

"Where do you work?"

"I don't, usually. I retired ten years ago. But a friend of mine asked me to mind his little boutique while he was on holiday. Today was my last day and I admit to giddy relief. No longer do I have to pretend to be some kind of sophisticated fashionista and can revert to my natural hippie state. What do you do?"

Beatrice considered the question. "I'm semi-retired. When I left the force – I was with the Metropolitan Police for over a decade – I set up a detective agency. It's hard to shake old habits, you know."

"How glamorous! A private investigator! Is it really glamorous or do you have to dig up grubby stories on royals and politicians?" Her brown eyes gleamed and Beatrice noticed her earrings, droplets of orange and green stone which picked up the notes in her patterned dress.

The waiter returned with a tray of delights. Two handled glasses filled with a dark liquid, the rims coated with caramelised sugar and topped with whipped cream, sat either side of a small silver plate carrying two decent-sized donuts, sprinkled with icing sugar.

Beatrice gave the waiter a big smile and snatched the bill to tuck into her shirt pocket. "How does one drink such a thing? Is there some kind of etiquette?"

Mia clasped her hands together in anticipation. "For the full combination of flavours, I recommend drinking it directly, unless you have an aversion to a cream moustache." She demonstrated, pinching the handle of one glass and raising it to her lips.

Beatrice copied her with rather less confidence, but found the brittle sugary edges and cold cream filtered the warm potent liquid, culminating in a wholly pleasurable event. "Good gracious! This is so much better than having a lie-down in my apartment. Thank you very much for introducing me to such an experience." She licked her lips.

"That's only the half of it. Next, we bite into a puff of air." She pushed the plate towards Beatrice who picked up one of the little cakes between finger and thumb. Out of politeness, she waited for Mia to go first.

The older woman still sported a line of cream across her top lip and bit into the doughnut with undisguised relish. She was exactly the kind of woman Beatrice liked.

They ate and drank with no other commentary than contented murmurs until the doughnuts were no more. Mia stirred the remaining cream into her special coffee and licked the spoon.

"This is my kind of afternoon tea," Beatrice exclaimed. "The coffee and cake distracted me from your question. No, I do not accept tabloid jobs seeking salacious material on public figures. The investigation agency belongs to me so I can pick and choose the jobs I want to take. No royals, no politicians, no tapping phones or scouring people's bins. To be truthful with you, there are precious few cases offered to me these days. Ooh, that rum has gone right to my head."

"That's the whole point. I've been hawking overpriced, mass-produced, poorly designed gear for the last two weeks and the only thing that kept me going was the thought of my Spanish coffee and bubble of air at the end of the day. I don't usually knock back two shots of hard liquor before the six o'clock news."

She laughed, a soft sound with an edge of mischief. "Are you staying for long?"

A pleasant warmth crept over Beatrice's skin. She gave her companion a broad smile. "Just over a week, I believe. We've rented the flat until next Friday. I'm here with two friends, Will and Adrian. We spent a week in Barcelona so Will could compete in the Iron Man challenge yesterday. This week, we're just chilling out by the beach. Or at least I am. Those two will probably cover more ground in seven days than I would do in a year. The joys of being young."

"There are just as many joys in being old. I'm going to be seventy-three next birthday and I embrace it. Don't you think we grow into ourselves? Fewer people to please, less pressure to be what we're not and a willingness to ..."

"Wear purple?"

Mia laughed, her shoulders shaking and hair rippling. "One of my favourite poems. I see it as my personal obligation to 'make up for the sobriety of my youth', don't you?"

"Yes, I suppose I do. Young Beatrice was an exceptionally sober youth, striving to excel in a male-dominated profession. I rarely let my hair down and when I did, I'd forgotten how."

With a sudden sharp focus, Mia reached her hand across the table to clasp Beatrice's wrist. "Do you have plans for tomorrow? Of course you do, silly question. It's just that tomorrow is a very special day in my town. I'd love to show it to someone for the first time."

Rum and recognition buzzed through Beatrice's veins. "Why not? My friends are going to Barcelona for lunch so I'm at a loose end. What's happening here tomorrow?"

She released Beatrice's wrist in order to gesticulate. "Not here, this is not my home town. I come from Vilanova i la Geltrú, the next stop down the train line. Tomorrow is Día de Sant Jordi, something everyone should experience once in their lives. It's a day for lovers, communities and stories. Men buy roses for their wives or girlfriends. Women buy books to give to their loved ones. Communities come together to play music and create human pyramids in the main square. The atmosphere is so unusual and respectful of every age. I think you would enjoy it, Beatrice. Why don't you join me and I'll show you around?"

Beatrice took another slug of coffee and made a decision. "That sounds exactly the sort of thing I would adore. Thank you, Mia, I would be delighted to have a local guide for such an authentic regional event."

"Wonderful! I will meet you at the train station and take you on a tour. We can have lunch and find ourselves a good spot for the main event. The weather is never predictable but my favourite café has umbrellas. When you're ready to go home, you just step on a train and arrive a few minutes later in Sitges. I'll give you my number in case of any confusion." She scribbled some digits on a beer mat.

"Old school," commented Beatrice, increasingly aware of the need to lie down. "Waiter? Can I settle up?"

Mia thanked her again and shook her hand as she got up to leave. "I'm very glad we met each other and I'm looking forward to tomorrow. Just let me know when you're on the train and I will meet you on the platform. Have a lovely evening, Beatrice and see you in the morning."

"Can't wait! Thank you for the invitation and the introduction to Spanish coffee. The boys are going to be so impressed!"

The boys were not impressed in the slightest. Will was appalled at her willingness to be taken in by a friendly stranger and questioned her judgement. Adrian, possibly with an ulterior motive, offered to accompany her rather than return to Barcelona with Will. That move annoyed Will to the point a full-scale row was about to erupt. Beatrice was slightly squiffy, very tired and in no mood for any kind of confrontation.

"Thank you for your concern. I am going to Vilanova whatsitsname on my own. Will, I am perfectly capable of taking care of myself and do not feel in the slightest taken in. For heaven's sake, the woman is seventy-two years old. Adrian, you may not use me as an excuse to get out of lunch with Manu and his family. You go to Barcelona, I am going to Vilanova. Now, I need a little lie down. If I'm not awake by the time you go for dinner, leave me a note and I will join you if I feel up to it." With her head held high, she stalked into the bedroom and lay down on top of the quilt, trying to remember the rest of the poem. Something about learning to spit?

3

When she awoke with the church bells, Beatrice was startled to realise that she had slept a full twelve hours. Her stomach was growling and her throat was dry. She tiptoed into the kitchen, drank a glass of water and boiled the kettle to make some coffee. In the light from the hob, she saw it was 6.15 am and the sun was yet to rise. On the table was a note from Will suggesting she meet them at Cinnamon, an Indian restaurant by the beach. That was ten hours ago.

Her conscience nudged her to make amends. She threw on yesterday's dress and a cardigan, slipped her feet into flip-flops, unlocked the door and went out to buy bread and pastries for breakfast. The streets were silent as the sky gradually changed from navy to grey, but the lights of the bakery drew in the early birds. Beatrice bought bread, milk and croissants and then walked down to one of the promenades to watch the sun rise. Hardly anyone was about other than a jogger on the beach and a dog walker aiding an ancient dachshund up the steps. The sunrise was, to Beatrice's mind, like going through a car wash. Everything fresh, cleansed and prepared for another day. She watched the colours develop, gnawing on a croissant and relaxing as if she were at home.

By the time she got back to the apartment, it was almost eight. Her companions were up and about, one in the shower and the other making scrambling eggs.

"So it's true what they say? Early to bed and early to rise. How are you feeling this morning?" Will wore a T-shirt and pyjama bottoms as he ground pepper into a pan.

"Fresh as a butternut! I've been out to buy provisions. Oh, Will, you should have seen the sunrise. Truly the most beautiful way to start a day. Although I am rather jealous of your Indian meal last night. Was it good?"

"So good you would not believe. We're definitely eating there again before we leave." Will looked into the paper bag of baked goods and sniffed. "Bread fresh from the oven, the most comforting smell in the world. Plus three croissants, one half eaten."

"Watching the dawn would make anyone peckish. Pass it over and I'll finish it with a hot cup of coffee. Have you and Adrian made your plans for the day?"

"Yes. We're going to Barcelona to lunch with Manu. I'm sorry for leaping to conclusions regarding your new friend. I hope you have a great time in Vilanova whatever. Just promise me you will keep your phone close at all times and call me if you feel in any way uncomfortable, yeah?"

"I promise. Are you two friends again?"

Adrian walked into the room wearing a Noel Coward style smoking jacket. "More than friends. In fact, we're thinking of renewing our vows. I smell coffee and if I'm not wrong, fresh bread. Were you up with the lark, PI Stubbs?"

Will served three portions of scrambled eggs, a slice of bread each and some grilled tomatoes. Beatrice abandoned her croissant and tucked into her cooked breakfast.

"I was! Therefore I go straight to the top of the Best Tourist leader board because I watched the sun come up. I don't suppose there's any brown sauce?"

Both men gave her a dry look.

"All right, all right. I'll just add more pepper. Do please give my best regards to Manu and let's debrief over dinner. I have a feeling today is going to be terrific fun."

The trip to Vilanova i la Geltrú took a matter of minutes. The train went through a couple of tunnels but mostly ran alongside the beach. If she'd been feeling madly energetic, she could have walked the coastal path. Perhaps she could propose it to Will and Adrian, so long as they made it a gentle stroll, not at Will's usual breakneck pace. Her phone buzzed and Beatrice saw Mia would be waiting for her at the train station. It felt refreshing to go exploring on her own, particularly as it was a location she had discovered under her own steam. She had a rebellious streak which urged her to keep learning, discovering and taking chances. She hoped she'd still be doing so at the age of seventy-two.

If Mia had looked stylish yesterday, she surpassed herself today. She wore a calf length Ikat-printed dress in shades of blue with nude suede wedges on her feet. Gone was the shopping trolley in favour of a navy shoulder bag. Silver filigree earrings dangled from her lobes and her wrists tinkled with the sound of stacked silver bracelets. A thick grey plait hung over one shoulder, a turquoise ribbon threaded into its folds. On seeing Beatrice, she lifted her sunglasses onto the top of her head and burst into welcoming smile.

"What did I tell you? Wasn't it easy?" She leaned forward and bumped her cheeks against Beatrice's. "*Benvinguts a Vilanova í la Geltrú*! I'm so pleased you came."

"So am I! Thank you for meeting me. I'm very excited about seeing something local. I must say, you look incredibly elegant. You'll have to give me some tips. I'm in very serious danger of becoming beige."

Mia tucked her arm into Beatrice's and they left the little station, threading their way past the waiting taxis and bus stops. "Beige has a role to play in everyone's wardrobe. Much like the chorus on the stage, it allows the star players to shine. I only thought to myself yesterday how well you wear natural fabrics. All we need is a splash of colour here and there. Let's cross the street and walk past the museum, it's quieter that way."

It soon became clear that Vilanova was extremely easy to navigate. They followed the street parallel to the railway and the beach, chatting comfortably. En route, they passed several queues of men standing outside flower shops.

"Buying roses for their beloveds, isn't it sweet? It's an old ritual and one I missed while living in England. Yes, you have Valentine's Day, but that is international and in my opinion, quite commercial. Día de St Jordi is more personal. You will see. Up here is the Rambla Principal."

Noise and a sense of energy built as they moved towards the main street. It was a broad pedestrianised thoroughfare with cafés either side of the street. All along the central strip, people strolled up and down, the majority accompanied by dogs, browsing small market stalls selling books. After a heightened sense of danger in Barcelona, Beatrice was wary of crowds. However, the community atmosphere reminded her of a Sunday market where the world came out to greet its neighbours.

Children, families, young couples, elderly groups of friends and occasional fake 'designer-handbag' sellers moved up and down in the street, frequently stopping for a chat or taking a break in one of the awning-shaded cafés. Halfway up one block stood two carved statues wearing mediaeval attire. The hubbub was too loud for Beatrice to make enquiries with Mia but she assumed the wooden gentleman wearing a beret was St Jordi, or St George in English. Hence the significance of the red roses.

The street stretched on and on with more cafés, more stalls, more people and more dogs. At the end, Beatrice could see a large square overlooked by a large pinkish-coloured church. Mia leaned across speak into her ear.

"My favourite café is just at the end by the post office. It's usually a little quieter than the places on the Rambla, but given today's festivities, I can offer no guarantee." She led the way past the church steps and into a triangular area where three streets met. In the centre was a fountain encircled by stone benches, shaded by trees. At the base of the triangle were three or four tables under an awning and a decorative sign saying *No és una perruqueria*. Beatrice would have assumed it was someone's house. The tables and chairs were mismatched and higgledy-piggledy, the doorway was covered by a curtain and the only clientele were two old men with a pair of Jack Russell terriers. On seeing Mia, the dogs started barking and the two men lifted their berets in greeting.

She waved and asked a question, provoking a laugh, then sat down two tables away.

"Beatrice, what would you like to drink? I thought we'd have a coffee break now then walk down to the main square for lunch. That way, we secure a prime position before the afternoon's entertainment. People can get very territorial when it comes to sightlines."

"Well, certainly not a Spanish coffee. After I left you yesterday afternoon, I went home, keeled over and slept until six am. On the bright side, I did see the sunrise. What are those chaps having?"

A woman emerged from the curtain to doorway in a grey smock, a pencil behind her ear. She gave every appearance of being hot, harassed and irritable, but when she saw Mia her frown dissipated and her brittle demeanour relaxed. The two women kissed one another on both cheeks and exchanged a few words in Catalan.

"Benet, I'd like to introduce you to my friend Beatrice. I'm sorry to speak English but Beatrice knows no Catalan. Beatrice, this is one of my oldest and dearest friends, Benet. She runs the best café in Vilanova í la Geltrú and taught me the secret of Spanish coffee."

Beatrice got to her feet and held out a hand. "In that case, I have a great deal to thank you for. After one Spanish coffee yesterday afternoon I slept a full twelve hours. I'm very pleased to meet you."

The corners of Benet's mouth raised a millimetre and she took Beatrice's hand in her own rough palm. "Same to you. You stay in Vilanova?"

"No, I'm staying in Sitges. That's where I met Mia."

The woman's expression didn't change. "Are you a gay?"

"Umm, no, I'm not a lesbian, but I am sharing my holiday apartment with two homosexuals if that makes a difference?"

Benet shrugged. "Makes no difference to me. Lesbians are smart. No one in their right mind would be with a man. What you want?"

The question threw Beatrice, but Mia came to her rescue. "We'll have *churros* and hot chocolate, please. Thank you, Benet."

It took several minutes after the woman returned inside before Beatrice could frame her question. "Is it normal for one's server to ascertain your sexuality before you order a drink?"

Mia laughed quietly but said nothing. A woman with a French bulldog walked past and the two Jack Russells launched a voluble attack, restrained by their leads. The owners of the dogs ignored the fracas and struck up a conversation. Mean-

while, a sleepy-looking teen placed two cups of steaming chocolate and a cinnamon-sprinkled tube between them.

Mia thanked the boy and took off her sunglasses. "It's funny
how you see your environment through different eyes when you
sit with a stranger. My friends from Spain found England and its
habits such a shock. They still talk about the breakfasts, the
fashions, the attitude to alcohol as if they had visited another
planet. With an Englishwoman at my table, I perceive how our
customs seem odd. Tradition says you dip the pastry in the
chocolate, but no one will judge you for eating it your way." She
tore the tube in two and passed half across the table. "I hope you
like it."

The scent of chocolatey milk distracted Beatrice from her
line of questioning. She followed Mia's lead, dabbed the crispy
dough into the hot chocolate and bit off the end.

"That is perfection. But unless I walk back to Sitges, I'll
never work off these calories."

"You will. We're going on a tour of the town, including the
castle and Pasifaë, the sculpture on the beach. By the time we
return to Plaça de la Vila, you'll be ready for the local speciali-
ty." Mia leaned over the table, her voice modulated. "Benet is
not anti-gay, just anti-husbands. Her first marriage ended in an
acrimonious divorce; her second in humiliation. She had one of
the best-known bars on the Rambla. Famous for its food and
cocktails. People travelled from Barcelona, Valencia, all over to
visit La Benet. Then her husband absconded with his hairdresser and all their money, leaving her with a mountain of
debts."

"What a shit!" Beatrice hissed.

"The shittiest of shits. Benet moved into her grandmother's
home and those two indomitable ladies built a quiet little café-
bar for those in the know. Her customers are hand-picked, the
address a secret to most people and when she makes her signa-

ture dish, the grapevine is hopping. It's a pity you're only here for a week."

Beatrice stirred her chocolate, looking at the fountain refracting light around the space. "It is. You have no idea how many places have tempted me to stay, but this one exerts an exceptional pull. Seaside, outdoor socialising, clement weather conditions and lots of dogs. Tell me, what's the meaning of the name?" She pointed to the sign: *No és una perruqueria*.

"Ah, that's another story, best told far from this little corner of town."

Mia guided her through streets, parks and markets with a constant stream of anecdotes, some personal, some historical. They stopped at little boutiques where Mia advised Beatrice to buy a chunky necklace, a duck-egg blue scarf, a pair of sage-green trousers, some crystal earrings and a cashmere wrap. Her advice was rational and every purchase made sense. Beatrice anticipated her next forays into Sitges or Upton St Nicholas looking so elegant and chic she would turn heads.

"Ach! I wanted to walk along the beach to Pasifaë, but the sun is at its worst. How are you feeling? Should we find ourselves a table in the main square and order an aperitif where you can parade your new jewellery? I know just the place."

The sun was indeed harsh and Beatrice was more than ready for a rest in the shade. "Show me the way. I also want to know the story about Benet's café. I know enough Spanish to understand the first bit. *No és una* means it's not. But what is it not?"

"*No és una perruqueria*. This is not a hair salon."

Beatrice stopped, overcome with laughter. "She called her café 'This is not a hair salon' after her husband ran off with his hairdresser? That is brilliant! My admiration for Benet just went through the roof! What a woman."

"She has incredible strength. We come from rival villages but I respect her more than most. Oh, Lord save us, the bands are tuning up. Let's take the long way around."

They ducked through groups wearing yellow shirts and white trousers with a black sash, parping on wind instruments, only to come across another collection of costumed musicians, this time wearing red tops. Mia was clearly a familiar figure, exchanging kisses, holding hands and patting shoulders. She waved a hand, beckoning Beatrice and the two women found a path onto Plaça de la Vila.

After all the narrow alleys and criss-crossing streets, the massive central square came as a shock. The scale of the place was staggering, the pattern of tiles too much to take in under the feet of the crowds and palm trees rustled in the April breeze.

"I took the liberty of booking a ringside seat," said Mia, indicating a lively restaurant with green umbrellas, subtle jazz emanating from the speakers and tables on two levels, offering all its patrons spectacular views. "You see more from upstairs but there's nothing quite like being close to the action. Year after year I've watched this event and it's always a tremendous buzz. I am so glad you're here to share it. You're a courageous woman, coming to a strange place with an even stranger woman. But now for the floor show which I know you will enjoy."

"I've enjoyed all of it so far," said Beatrice, without exaggeration. "You're extremely kind to share your city's secrets with me." She tucked her bags beneath the table and relaxed into her seat to survey the square. "I'm surprised you could bear to leave such a place. I have nothing against Salisbury, but Vilanova is a revelation."

Mia gave a sad smile. Thank you. I admit I'm happy to be home. Shall we have an Aperol Spritz to whet our appetites? Then I'll ask about the Special of the Day because this place pulls out all the stops on Día de Sant Jordi. Are you going to try your new jewellery? I can't wait to see how it works with your wrap."

"Good idea. I'll nip to the loo and bedeck myself in my new finery. Whatever the special of the day is, order one for me. I'll eat anything."

A few minutes in the bathroom provided the opportunity to reassure Will she was still alive. After washing her hands and debating whether to wear the scarf or the necklace, she took a selfie and sent it to both Will and Adrian, with the caption 'Fashionista Stubbs dines out in style! Hope you're having fun too. Bxx'

When she returned to the table, Mia widened her eyes. "What did I tell you? That necklace adds so much to your outfit you should pay it overtime. The earrings work wonders, catching the light without dominating, but sending a message that says stand back, everyone, here is one classy lady. Here's to your new image! Cheers!"

They raised their orange-coloured glasses.

"With grateful thanks to my stylist," said Beatrice, who could not stop grinning. "Mmm, that's very refreshing. What are we having for lunch?"

"I ordered us a tapas sampler so we can taste a little bit of everything. It's early for most people to eat lunch, but I want to be able to concentrate on the pyramids when they start."

A young woman wearing a black apron over a white shirt placed a large platter in the centre of the table, filled with thrilling little curiosities. Beatrice admired a sensible plate. None of this slate or breadboard foolishness where all the contents might easily slide to the floor.

"Mia, you read my mind. This is exactly my kind of lunch! *Buen provecho*! Now tell me about these pyramids." She placed an anchovy and cube of tortilla on her plate, alongside a breadstick.

"I can tell you the bare facts, but you will have to see the reality to appreciate why it is so important to this region. Vilanovins have a reputation for being party magpies, much like English-speakers fill their dictionaries with words appropriated from other languages. If there's a festival going on, Vilanova wants a part of it. Because of our history, there's a deeper principle behind this willingness to celebrate at the drop of a hat. Vilanova i la Geltrú has always welcomed newcomers, whether Spanish fugitives from Franco's regime or refugees from unstable regions in the rest of the world. It's not just Vilanova but the whole Catalonian region which promotes *convivencia*, best translated as living together as a community. Festivals are the cornerstone of that. Pageants, good-natured battles, satirical comment on one's overlords, it's a way of people coming together and respecting our neighbours. It helps that many redraw the lines of identity. Plus most of the *festas* involve eating. Catalonia loves food."

"I can see why. One thing you said I don't quite understand. 'Redraw the lines of identity'? How do you mean? Will you please eat something so I don't look like an appalling hog?"

"Yes, sorry. I was too busy talking. That happens a lot." Mia popped olives and peppers into her mouth and gnawed on a breadstick. "Lines of identity. Let me ask you a question. Who are you? Who do *you* think you are?"

Beatrice stopped eating. "I'm a semi-retired woman in her sixties who loves dogs and likes anchovies."

"A-ha. So if we gathered everyone in this square and asked each to form a unit, you would join the fish aficionados? Or would you gravitate to older people with fabulous jewellery? Perhaps you'd rush over to the white women's corner where they serve glasses of Chardonnay? Then you could choose to apply for membership of the white-with-brown-eyes sub-group and ally yourself with Yorkshire Terrier Appreciation Society. I'm joking, Beatrice, but that's what I mean by lines of identity. Villages or communities in Catalonia generate events where everyone participates. On Día de la Dona, all women from toddlers to great-grandmothers, white, black, Latin, lesbian, Catalan, Castilian, cat-ladies, dog-lovers, pigeon-fanciers and everything in between are embraced. People who call each other sister or brother then become fierce opponents during the village football match, or try to outdo one another during the Carnaval parades. We are convivial, acknowledging the many things that bring us together and bridging the few that keep us apart. Today is the day of the villages. Each one of these little communities has spent a year practising the *castello*, or human tower. I tend to get sentimental about such things, but to me, today is a symbol of society at its best." Her eyes were flooded with tears.

Beatrice reached across the table, fighting the impulse to defuse the moment with a wisecrack. "That was wonderfully put. I appreciate the insight. You are a lucky woman to have grown up with such a culture."

Mia clasped Beatrice's hand and dabbed at her eyes with her napkin. "Excuse me, you must think me madly eccentric. I have a few close friends with whom I cry unashamedly but you and I only just met. I apologise. Maybe I can make up for it by taking you to a karaoke bar and doing my Dolly Parton. Why are you laughing?"

"Because you may be a Vilanovin but you have a British carapace. I restrained myself from cracking a joke but you got there first. Defuse the emotion and raise a laugh, that's part of our DNA." Beatrice released her hand and picked up her glass. "Whatever your cultural make-up, I am very glad we met."

Mia's response was drowned out by the musicians entering the square. To Beatrice's untrained eye, it all seemed a bit of a muddle. Bands marched in from all directions, playing competing tunes as they mingled with the crowds. She had no idea where to look but it seemed the majority of red or yellow clad performers were making for the building opposite. They clustered in large groups, shouting and jostling so that from a distance it could be mistaken for a fight. Then some sort of order prevailed and a circle of men in red shirts climbed up to stand on the shoulders of a group of men below. All around them were a tightly packed crowd, holding onto the men's legs in support.

Next, four more barefoot men scrambled up, using the second level's sashes as toe holds and formed a third layer, clasping one another's arms. Onto their shoulders clambered four women. By now the men forming the base were bearing the weight of twelve people and the necessity of the supporting crowd became obvious. Two girls made their way to the top of the tower to stand on the women's shoulders, faced one another and grasped arms. The whole thing was beginning to shake slightly at this stage. Then two tiny girls around eight years old, both wearing helmets, scaled the human structure with all the determination of seasoned mountaineers. The first placed her hands and feet on the shoulders of the teenagers, level with the spectators on the balcony. The second crawled on top of her teammate like a crab and raised her arm in the air. The breathless audience burst into applause and the girls began their descent. Watching the red and white pyramid dismantle itself was almost as fascinating as seeing it go up.

Beatrice joined in the applause with gusto, touched by such a display of cooperation and courage. "Those little girls are so brave! That must be ten metres high and quite terrifying for one so young."

"Aren't they wonderful? We call them squirrels. I could never have done such a thing at that age and have nothing but admiration for those gutsy kids."

"For all of them, really. I completely understand what you

mean about a social bonding event. I'm bursting with pride and I don't know any of these people."

"There will be at least half a dozen over the next hour, so that was just the beginning. What do you say ordering to a bottle of wine? We can continue grazing as we watch the entertainment."

"I'd say that's an excellent plan. Which one of these groups is your village?"

"I come from Sirenes, a small place about five kilometres west of here on the Foix River. The villagers are wearing yellow but I'm not sure when their turn will be. As for the choice of wines, is a bottle of Penedès acceptable? It's a local product which can match the strong tastes of tapas."

"Local sounds good to me."

After Mia had relayed their order to the waitress, Beatrice had a question. "On Thursday after the triathlon, we had a glass of some very good local fizz, but I don't recall the name. It wasn't cava, but I think it began with a C."

"Corpinnat? That's a very good choice. It's …" Before she could continue, another pyramid began at the nearest end of the square, this time with a group all dressed in canary yellow. Mia gasped in excitement. "This is my village!"

The *castello* crew were much closer this time. Beatrice forgot about her grilled courgettes as all her attention was consumed by the physical efforts of the group in yellow. The bottom tier of men was well chosen, each as stocky and muscular as a bull and all of a similar height. No sooner were they in position than a three-deep circle of people surrounded them, reinforcing the base. From that group emerged the second rung, heaving themselves onto the shoulders of the first. At this distance, Beatrice could see their expressions differed from those of the delighted crowd. The *castello*-building men were serious and responsible, with a touch of fear.

The wine arrived and Mia told the girl to pour, too absorbed in the pyramid to bother with tasting. Unlike the red team, the yellows worked in groups of three, not four. A trio of lighter males took their place, gripping one another's shoulders and one gave a signal of readiness to the three women who climbed the men's backs as if they were trees. Once in position, the two teenage girls used their knees, feet, elbows and hands to ascend. Close up, it looked painful for the lower layers and Beatrice could well imagine the bruises sustained.

One of the girls missed her footing and slid down her neighbours as if she were on a greasy pole. Groans came from the observers but the support team on the ground broke her fall and pushed her upwards. Showing enormous pluck, the girl tried again and made it into position with the sympathetic encouragement of the crowd. She clutched her team mate's arms and nodded to indicate she was ready. The two little squirrels, as Mia had called them, started scrambling up the tower.

That was when something gave way. A man on the second tier crumpled, falling backwards into the crowd to horrified gasps. The foundations gone, the rest of the pyramid wobbled and fell, collapsing onto one another like a house of cards. The sound of bodies hitting bodies from a height was sickening. Like everyone else, Beatrice's immediate instinct was to run and help, but she stopped at the sound of a police whistle. This was a matter for the emergency services. Ambulance sirens echoed around the square, amplified by the tall buildings on every side, forcing many people to cover their ears.

Almost every patron of the café was either crossing themselves or praying, Mia clapped her hands to her face, a frozen version of Munch's *The Scream*, and the waitress stood open-mouthed, shedding silent tears.

A loudspeaker began issuing orders, unintelligible to Beatrice, but Mia grabbed her arm. "The police want everyone to leave the square immediately. Go to the station. Don't forget your bags. I'm so sorry." She left the table and disappeared into the crowd.

In a shocked daze, Beatrice gathered her things, left €50 under her plate and joined the hordes of people filing into the narrow streets. She was too stunned to cry.

4

Once safely home in the Sitges apartment, a sense of duty impelled her to send Will and Adrian a text message. She could think of no succinct way to explain why she had cut short her trip, so she made no reference to the upsetting events in the square.

Home safe. Hope you're having fun. Bx

She dithered over whether or not to call Mia but eventually decided against. The poor woman would have enough to do assisting her fellow villagers and comforting the relatives of those wounded. Beatrice could only pray those injuries were minor and nothing worse had happened. There was no way she could check on the news because she didn't understand Spanish. In frustration, she paced the apartment, pouring a glass of water, sitting in the kitchen, getting up again, picking up a book and putting it down again until she started to get on her own nerves.

The sound of her mobile ringing gave her a start. She snatched it up in the hope it was Mia but saw Adrian's name on the display.

"Hello, Adrian. How was lunch?"

"Lovely. We're just walking it off with a stroll around the park, but I thought I'd give you a quick call. Why are you home so early? Did you have fun?"

Beatrice opened her mouth but found she couldn't answer.

"Beatrice? Are you all right?"

"I'm fine, absolutely fine. Oh, Adrian, the most dreadful thing happened and I don't know how bad it is because I can't read the news and I don't want to bother Mia and I'm just pacing around and fretting."

"My God? What was it?"

Beatrice told him as coherently as she could manage but failed to deliver the full horror of seeing those people fall on top of one another. She just said, "It was awful, too awful for words."

"You poor thing! What a nasty shock you must have had. Look, Will and I will get the next train back to Sitges. You shouldn't be alone at a time like this. We'll say our goodbyes to Manu and his wife and be with you as fast as we can."

Beatrice closed her eyes with relief then opened them again sharply. "No! I need to know how serious it was and there must be something on the news. Manu speaks Spanish so surely he will know how to discover any information? Could you ask him to check? I'm desperate to know no one was badly hurt."

"Good idea. I'll ask him to find out what he can and call us with an update. Try not to worry too much. We are on our way."

"Thank you, Adrian, I have no idea what I'd do without you. See you shortly."

On ending the call, she felt a good deal calmer at the thought of her companions' return. There was nothing to be achieved by hanging around the apartment, so she stuffed her phone into her handbag and went out into the streets. She had an urge to be around people, to stroll in the sunshine and remind herself of normality.

That lasted for approximately five minutes. All these people shopping for trinkets, drinking wine outside cafés and laughing as if they hadn't a care in the world irritated her and made her bad tempered. She walked down to the beach, hoping Nature would prove restorative and soothe her fractious mood. Even before she approached the café where she had met Mia, she had made up mind not to stop for a drink. As it turned out, she had no choice. All the tables and chairs were occupied. She sat on the sea wall. Waves rolled up the beach, chasing little children up the sand. Endearing as the scene appeared, high-pitched squeals jarred her nerves. She gave up trying to take her mind off what had happened and turned in the direction of the apartment.

Her phone rang and the display showed an unknown number. She answered, stepping off the main thoroughfare and into a little alley.

"Hello?"

"Hello, Beatrice. This is Manuel. Adrian gave me your number."

"Manu! Thank you so much for calling."

"You're welcome. I understand you were in Vilanova i la Geltrú this afternoon and saw the accident. Are you okay?"

"I'm fine. Well, a little shaken, and obviously very worried about the people involved. Have you heard any news?"

"There's not much information available because it only happened a couple of hours ago. The police just made a statement. They don't know the reason the pyramid collapsed but six people have been taken to hospital, two of whom are in a critical condition. They are going to give a further update at nine o'clock this evening. I'll watch the report and call you afterwards to tell you what they say."

"Six! Oh dear, that's so awful. Thank you for letting me know. I really would appreciate a call later this evening if there are any developments. Thank you Manu, you are most kind."

"It's nothing, Beatrice, don't mention it. Why don't you have a glass of brandy and sit somewhere out of the sun until your friends return? We'll speak later. Goodbye."

She wished him a good evening and saw a message from Adrian. He and Will were due to arrive in Sitges in just over an hour. Although Manu's advice was aimed at a delicate old lady, rather than a capable woman like herself, Beatrice decided to take it. The little alleyway in which she stood had steps going down in the direction of the beach and halfway along there was a little landing with just enough space for two small café tables. It looked exactly her kind of place. She walked down the shady half of the street, ordered in the café and seated herself at one of the two outside tables. It was strange. Normally she liked the hustle and bustle of the main promenade, a wonderful place for people watching. But today the silence and feeling of finding a hideaway was exactly what she needed.

Two people in a critical condition. The little girls would have had the furthest to fall yet they had only just begun their ascent when the second tier collapsed. Therefore the people at the top would have been the pair of teenagers. Yet it was not only the people forming the pyramid itself at risk. Those at the bottom, supporting the legs of the men and forming a human safety net were directly in the path of danger. The sound of bodies smacking into one another with force ricocheted through her ears and she winced. The bar owner emerged with her coffee and brandy.

"You cold, *señora*? You want I put the table in the sunshine?"

"No, thank you, I'm not cold. I like the shade. Thank you very much."

"OK. Enjoy." He placed her drinks on the paper tablecloth and wandered up the steps to the main street, where he leant against the wall and lit a cigarette.

There was no point in hypothesising about what had

happened. As her mother often used to say 'Worry when it happens, otherwise you may worry in vain'. Poor Mia! To see her friends and family suffer such an appalling ordeal; she was probably inconsolable. The coffee and the brandy soon took effect and Beatrice's mind settled into a calm patience. Her eyes rested on the bill and another worry floated to the surface.

She hadn't even seen the menu in the restaurant Plaça de la Vila. Two Aperol Spritzes, a tapas tasting-platter and a half a bottle of wine – would fifty euros cover it? She would look it up online and if she discovered she had underpaid she would send them a note in the post. Because the last thing she felt like doing was going back to Vilanova.

The shade of the building now stretched across the entire alleyway and the breeze blowing up from the sea had an edge to it. Beatrice left the money for her drink, plus a tip, in the saucer of her coffee cup and said goodbye to the owner who was still watching passers-by at the top of the steps. As she passed the supermarket, she considered buying something for dinner as going out to a restaurant that evening held no appeal. But then neither did queuing at the checkout with a handful of mismatched products they might never eat. She headed for their temporary home instead.

"There you are! I was just about to call you." Adrian rushed out of the kitchen to hug Beatrice. She squeezed him tight, grateful for his familiar citrusy perfume and reassuring embrace.

"Have you heard from Manu? He rang while we were on the train."

"Yes. He was kind enough to fill me in and promised to do so again when there's more news. Did you have a nice lunch?"

Will stood in the kitchen doorway, his expression concerned. "It was excellent. But how about you? How do you feel?"

"A bit steadier now, but still worried, upset and completely useless. I know there's nothing I can do but when you see something like that first hand, you feel a sense of responsibility."

"That's only natural. I expect your friend took it even harder. Wasn't it her idea to watch the spectacle?"

"Not just her idea, but it was her village! The people who fell were her friends and neighbours. Poor thing must be absolutely devastated. I can barely imagine."

Adrian guided her to the sofa and placed a glass of iced water on a coaster. "You mean you didn't speak to her after the event?"

Beatrice sipped and shook her head. "No, I didn't get chance. The police were clearing everyone out of the square. It was mayhem, with sirens and screams and confusion. I snatched up my stuff, as she told me to do, and hurried away in the middle of hordes of shocked and traumatised people. I don't know where she went. Probably to help, I suppose. It took me over half an hour to regain orientation and work out where the station was. I haven't contacted her in any way because she has enough on her plate. I'll wait to hear from Manu first, and send a message tomorrow morning. It was so close to us." She looked up at Will. "I've seen worse and so have you in the line of duty, but this was completely unexpected. Up until that moment, it had been a lovely day. Mia showed me the city and explained the traditions behind the festival, we did some frivolous shopping, laughed over coffee and cried over lunch and then wham! It was right in front of us. I could hear them falling." She covered her eyes with a hand, trying block out the images and sounds.

"Beatrice, you've had a shock. Not just what you saw, but being out of your environment, unable to understand the language and separated from your friends. You'll need time to process all this. You know you can lean on us. Adrian and I are willing to either listen or change the subject, whatever you prefer. I guess you'd rather not go out on the town tonight. Shall I cook us something light for dinner and we can watch a movie? Just to take your mind off things until Manu calls."

"That sounds exactly what I need. Sorry to bring everyone down."

"You're not bringing anyone down. I'm still knackered after Thursday and could do with a night lounging on the sofa. I'm going to source some fresh veg and I expect an ice-cold gin and tonic on my return. Do I make myself clear, Mr Harvey?"

"Crystal, DI Quinn. Coming right up. Beatrice, come keep me company in the kitchen and tell me more about this 'frivolous shopping'. I saw all those bags and couldn't believe it. Not in all the years we've been friends have you shown the slightest interest in frivolity."

They ate artichokes with salted cod and watched *Women on the Verge of a Nervous Breakdown* in Spanish with English subtitles. A perfect choice. Beatrice laughed aloud on several occasions. When the film was over, Adrian and Will talked enthusiastically about Pedro Almodovar and his oeuvre. Beatrice picked at the food and listened, entertained by their passionate opinions. She tended to side with Adrian. Not that she had any real familiarity with the director's work but she was positively surprised by his depiction of women. She asked them to make a list of his other films so she could expand her education.

It was only half past eight but Beatrice was already getting edgy. She'd refused a glass of wine with dinner and a coffee afterwards, concerned about disruption to her sleep. Will's phone rang and he took it into the bedroom to answer the call. Meanwhile Beatrice and Adrian cleared away the dinner things. He did everything he could to distract her, suggesting tours and tastings for the following few days, but Beatrice's concentration was shot.

After a few minutes, Will returned to the living room, carrying his laptop. His face indicated bad news.

"That was Manu. Facts about the Vilanova accident are now available in English. A police representative spoke to the press ten minutes ago. Three people have been discharged from hospital; two teenagers remain under observation but are no longer critical. Unfortunately a thirty-two year old woman has died of her injuries. A man arrested under suspicion of sabotage has been released. You can read for yourself." He handed over the laptop, took the wine bottle and motioned to Adrian. They retreated to the balcony, murmuring in low voices as Beatrice scrolled and read and clicked and tried to make sense of the news.

She spent almost two hours reading the same information in different ways until Adrian came to sit beside her.

"Time for bed, don't you think? You can check again in the morning."

Beatrice closed the machine and looked from him to Will, who was sitting on the arm of the sofa. "I think I want to go home. You have another week of holiday and I'll only spoil it by wandering around like a wet blanket. Also, I want to be in my own bed, with Huggy Bear snoring beside me. Don't even think about cutting your holiday short. I will be perfectly fine to travel alone. First thing in the morning, I'll book myself a flight."

Adrian stroked her shoulder. "If that's what you want, of course you must go. Why not sleep on it and see how you feel? Tomorrow is Sunday. Will and I were thinking of taking a trip to the Corpinnat vineyard and having a tasting menu. It might take your mind off things. There will be more flights on Monday, too. Shall we discuss it in the morning?"

"All right. I doubt I'll change my mind, but it never hurts to reconsider in the cold light of day. Thank you for being such bricks. Goodnight, sleep tight, hope the hedgehogs don't bite."

5

Despite a troubled night's sleep, Beatrice awoke feeling a lot better than the previous day. She lay in bed for a while, as was her wont, talking it over with Matthew. Since losing the love of her life, she had got into the habit of visiting the bench constructed in his memory and pouring out all her worries, just as she had always done when he was alive. She wouldn't go as far as to say she felt his presence, all patient attention and good sense, but the very act of telling him what bothered her had a soothing effect. Sitges was a long way from their village, but she told him anyway. With her eyes closed, she pictured his face, listening, his brow creased in thought. His voice seemed to come from somewhere within.

I am not in the slightest bit surprised you were upset, Old Thing. Enough to give anyone the heebie-jeebies. Not sure how rushing home on the first flight will make a difference, but you should do what you feel is best. Perhaps a few quieter days in the countryside would do the trick. After all, you do love a vineyard.

"That is true. I think I have the tiniest aversion to crowds after Barcelona and what happened yesterday. Maybe I will stay another day. I can always fly home on Monday. Thank you, my love. Talking to you makes me feel so much better."

She swung herself out of bed and located her phone. Her first priority was to send condolences to Mia. Then she went into the bathroom, thinking about the other man who always made her feel better. Her appointments with her therapist were now on an ad hoc basis, if and when she needed to unpack a particular issue. This counted as exactly that. Even so, she ought to spend a few days processing the incident herself, rather than rushing off to James. Why did she always need someone else to tell her what to think? Whilst in the shower, she practised describing the accident with a focus on facts above emotions. It gave her some distance.

In the kitchen, Adrian and Will were already having breakfast. As usual, Will was poring over a map and Adrian was scrolling through his phone.

"Good morning, you two. Do I smell coffee?" she asked.

"Good morning, Beatrice. How did you sleep? Take a seat and I'll make yours just the way you like it." Adrian planted a kiss on her cheek.

"Better than I expected. I had a little think after I woke up. On balance I might stay on, at least another day, if that's all right with you." She didn't mention her imaginary conversations with Matthew or James. Certain things were no one else's business but her own. "After all, I do love a vineyard."

"That is excellent news!" Will turned the map towards her and pointed out the distance between their apartment in Sitges and the Corpinnat vineyard. "Public transport is tricky and a taxi is going to cost us, so I thought I'd hire a car. I'm not bothered about drinking and I love to take the wheel so we can see a little more of the region. I reckon we should leave here about eleven, take the tour at twelve and book seats in the restaurant for two o'clock. That means a good five hours before your next meal, so get some toast down your neck."

Adrian handed her a mug of milky coffee and two slices of rustic toast. "Only happy when he's planning. There's butter, jam, cheese and some of that ham we bought in Barcelona. Are you going to wear your new clothes and jewellery today? I can't think of a better location for you to swan about and flash your sense of style."

It was an appealing thought. A change is as good as a rest and no matter how old she got, change was always appealing. She was about to reply in the affirmative when her phone rang. She glanced at the display and took the phone and coffee onto the balcony.

"Mia! How are you? Did you get my message?"

"Yes, I did. I have just picked up my handbag at the police station. It got lost in the confusion yesterday afternoon but someone very kindly found it and handed it in. My phone, my keys, my purse and all my cards are intact. That's why I haven't called you before, because I didn't have your number. I'm so sorry for abandoning you like that. I hope you got home without incident."

"Don't give it a second thought! I've been worrying about you and the people of your village since we parted. A friend of mine was kind enough to translate the news. I'm so deeply sorry about the woman who lost her life. Sorry for everyone who has been affected." An unpleasant thought occurred to her. "Have there been further developments overnight?"

"Further developments? That depends what you mean. Listen, Beatrice, would you have time for a coffee at some point today? There's something I'd like to share with you. I can come to Sitges if that's more convenient?"

Beatrice glanced into the kitchen where Adrian was buttering more toast. "Today might be difficult because my friends and I are planning to visit a vineyard. I'm not sure what time we will be back. Is it something you can tell me over the phone?"

For a moment, Beatrice could hear nothing but seagulls and the faint sound of traffic. "Mia? Are you still there?"

"I'm still here. What time do you leave for your tour? I can be in Sitges by ten o'clock and there's a café opposite the station where we can talk. Could you spare me half an hour? This is important to me otherwise I would not intrude upon your holiday. Please, Beatrice, I value your opinion."

Beatrice glanced at her watch and thought for a moment. "I'm sure that won't be a problem. What's the name of the café?"

"La Paloma." She gave a little laugh. "The name is appropriate. It's loud and brash and brazenly opportunistic, just like a pigeon. I'll see you there at ten. Thank you, my friend."

Will was wearing his sunglasses as he bought Beatrice's toast and a cafetière onto the balcony, but the Ray-Bans did not disguise his enquiring look.

"That was Mia. She wants to talk. Would it be OK if I went to meet her near the train station and caught up with you in time to leave at eleven?"

"You don't need to ask my permission. What does she want to talk about? Eat your toast, it's getting cold."

"Dunno yet. She didn't give much away. Maybe this is a bad idea." She bit into her toast and stared out at the ocean view. "If it's about yesterday, I'm not sure I want to hear it."

"Here are your options," said Will, topping up her coffee mug. "One: go and listen to what she has to say. Two: call back and say you can't make it. Blame it on your boot camp gay friends. Three: take a police detective with you as backup. Four: employ surveillance. Adrian and I could arrive at the café fifteen minutes before you and choose the right table from where we can see everything. Two gay men in a café will hardly raise eyebrows in Sitges. We prearrange a signal, such as dropping a teaspoon, which means 'come rescue me'. I might be recovering from the whole Iron Man experience, but I reckon I can take a seventy-two-year-old."

Beatrice spluttered toast crumbs over the table. "Don't be ridiculous. Why on earth would I want you and Adrian to play The A-Team? She's a nice woman and she wants to talk. I'll be finished and ready for our vineyard tour by eleven o'clock. Where is Adrian, by the way?"

"Emergency shopping. His outfit was not complete without the woven bracelet he was ogling two days ago. Between you and me, I'm not sure it was only the bracelet he was ogling. Seriously, Beatrice, we're picking up the hire car from the station. If you want me to lurk in the background, you only have to say the word. Otherwise, we'll leave as arranged for a luxury lunch at the vineyards by eleven. You'd better get dressed."

At five minutes to eleven, a sophisticated female sat at a table outside La Paloma café. In pale-green trousers, a neutral shirt accessorised with a jewel-coloured silk scarf and crystal earrings, she projected an air of nonchalance. Behind her sunglasses, she studied every other piece of passing footwear, concerned that her sturdy trainers would give her away as an amateur. No one seemed to notice and she ordered a glass of water as if she dressed this way every day.

Mia crossed the street with a wave, a large-brimmed hat shading her eyes. She wore dark jeans and a gold trimmed poncho with blue suede wedges, making Beatrice feel as glamorous as a napkin.

"You're here!" Mia kissed her on both cheeks, followed by a warm embrace. "I thought you'd never speak to me again after I abandoned you. Thank you so much for meeting me. The last twenty-four hours have been such a roller-coaster! A happy morning showing you my city, the nightmare of the afternoon and a long night's vigil for everyone in my village. No one escaped unscathed and everyone is grieving." She waved a hand at the bar and somehow wordlessly ordered a coffee. "For you as well. What an introduction to my town! I'm sorrier than I can say."

"Not your fault, Mia. It was an accident."

Mia said nothing, staring at the tablecloth until the waiter placed a thimbleful of coffee and a glass of water on the table. Beatrice noticed her saucer contained one of those nice mini chocolates you didn't get with a boring mineral water.

"It was an accident. The words on everyone's lips. So sad, it happens, what can we do? Today, I heard from an old friend in the police force. The cause of the accident was one man. He passed out and fell from the second layer. One single element of the support structure collapses, the whole thing goes down. Broken bones, bruised bodies and poor Núria lost her life."

"Oh God." Beatrice covered her face with her hands.

"I'm sorry. It's reliving the nightmare, I understand. But I am determined to relive it again and again until I understand what really happened. That's why I need your help."

Beatrice took off her sunglasses and stared. "My help? Why me? I know nothing about the situation and to be honest, had every intention of flying out of here as soon as possible after witnessing that shocking incident. My sympathies are with you and all those affected by this tragedy, but I'm a tourist who can't even speak the language. You've got the wrong woman."

Mia lifted her sunglasses in a matching gesture. Her eyes were puffy but focused. "No, they've got the wrong man."

Her conviction struck Beatrice with some force. She took another sip of water, considered paying the bill and saying goodbye, but something about her statement required clarification.

"I have to leave in the next few minutes, so please make this quick. Who is the wrong man?"

"The man who fainted is called Bertrand Gallego. He's a local legend, the village football coach and one of the pageant directors. He's taken part in the *castellos* for the last ten years and everyone knows him. In hospital he was treated for cuts and abrasions plus a broken finger. They tested his blood and found him under the influence of alcohol. Like, four times over the limit."

Over the other side of the street, Will idled by a kiosk, browsing magazines he couldn't understand.

"In that case, I understand your distress." Beatrice leaned forward to meet Mia's eyes. "For a pillar of the community to get drunk and let everyone down ..." she stopped and cringed at her choice of words. "For someone you trust to behave irresponsibly is a betrayal, but especially when that behaviour costs lives. I sympathise, truly I do, but other than echoing your sentiments, there's nothing I can say or do to help."

"You told me you are a private detective." Mia held her gaze.

"Was. I was a detective. I am now mostly retired and having a nice little holiday with some friends before I return to my cottage in Devonshire. Probably tomorrow morning."

Mia drank her coffee and slugged her water. "That's a pity. It was nice to meet you and I hope you have a lovely time at the vineyard. I'll get the bill because you paid for lunch. Safe journey home."

Her polite dismissal got under Beatrice's skin. "That's very kind. I appreciate your friendship and all the fashion tips." She flapped her scarf.

"It works, doesn't it? Pop of colour under the chin draws the attention to the face. But maybe a darker lip colour for winter? Berry red, I recommend."

Beatrice stood up and opened her arms for an embrace. "I'm

so sorry about what happened and I'd like to send a donation to the village, if that's appropriate. Would you let me know? I wish I could have been more use, but there really is no case."

Mia stepped backwards, her jaw set. "How do you know? You said yourself you understand nothing about us, our customs and our people. Neither do the police. This is why Bertrand will carry the blame for the whole village of Sirenes when he is innocent."

Will crossed the road and ordered a bottle of water at the bar, subtly reporting for duty.

"You're right, Mia, I know nothing about your culture, customs and village personalities. If you think there's something to explore, hire a local PI or someone who speaks the language, at the very least. Why are you so convinced this man is innocent?"

"Bertrand Gallego never preaches but encourages the footballers to avoid beer, sets up tournaments where everybody drinks water and opposes the culture of alcohol equals enjoyment. Bertrand is and always has been teetotal."

"So why did he collapse under the influence of drink?" asked Beatrice.

"That's what I want you to tell me. Beatrice, we need your help."

6

The vineyard's location, nestled into a hillside with forests at the rear and sweeping fields all around, boasted spectacular views of the Catalonian countryside. On the blue-tinted horizon rose a range of mountains shaped like sharp teeth. In the middle distance clustered small villages linked by convoluted roads. Meadows filled with spring flowers rippled in the Mediterranean breeze, their wildness in contrast to the regimented rows of vines. The winery itself was an architectural delight, a mixture of whitewashed houses with tiled roofs and roses climbing the walls, alongside adobe-style outbuildings in colours of terracotta and sandstone. It was a family-run business and had the air of being someone's home. In a lean-to garage covered with clematis, a car and child's bike were visible. A brindle cat lounged on a wooden bench outside the door.

Will parked in the visitors' bay and they walked up the drive to meet their host. Another tour party was coming in the other direction, led by a guide speaking French, who broke off to wish them a good morning in English. Beatrice, Adrian and Will returned the greeting.

"How did he know?" Adrian hissed once they were out of earshot.

"That we were Brits?" asked Will.

"Exactly. I do my best to dress like a European. Look at me! Jumper over my shoulders, check. Brown shoes with jeans, check. No unsightly lumps in trousers because my wallet and phone are in my man bag. Beatrice looks like a classic city sophisticate from Seville or San Sebastian. So how did he know?"

Will shrugged. "Probably their policy to greet everyone in English because it's the lingua franca. I wouldn't take it personally."

"Unless it's your haircut?" said Beatrice, as innocently as she could manage.

Adrian stopped in his tracks. "What's wrong with my haircut?"

"Nothing. Only in my experience of working in Europe, people say they can always identify a Brit by the hairstyle."

"Beatrice, stop winding him up," said Will. "Here's our guide. Hi! You must be Montserrat. We're the Quinn party. My name is Will, my husband is called Adrian and this our friend, Beatrice."

A middle-aged woman in a deep purple dress accessorised with a pink shawl gave them a pleasant smile. Her make-up was impeccable. "Good morning! I'm very pleased to meet you all. You're having a winery tour and staying with us for lunch, is that correct?"

"Correct. We're looking forward to it."

"Excellent! Then let's get started."

Montserrat was a superb guide. Her delivery was no learned-by-rote series of facts, but a story told by an expert narrator. She paused often, as if anticipating questions. She was not disappointed. Adrian monopolised the woman, eager to learn the more complex elements of soil structure and climate change on the harvest. Some of the technical detail went over Beatrice's head but she enjoyed strolling amongst the vines, examining the grapes and admiring the viniculturist's skills. It reminded her of another vineyard tour she had done in Spain. The one where she'd broken her nose.

"The grape varieties come from three separate vineyards, the oldest of which dates back to 1934. This is a Macabeu, which can be picked early and blended with other components, but is at its best after a long dry autumn. It is an essential ingredient for both Cava and Corpinnat."

"More than Xarel-lo?" Adrian enquired.

Montserrat raised an elegant eyebrow. "You know your wines, Mr Quinn."

"Thank you. It's not actually Mr Quinn but Mr Harvey. My husband and I kept our own names, you see. I'm Adrian Harvey of Harvey's Wine Emporium, Dionysus et al. Anyway, please call me Adrian."

"All right, Adrian. Which other grapes would you expect to find in a Corpinnat?"

Will and Beatrice fell behind as Adrian and Montserrat discussed names Beatrice had never heard of.

"He's in his element," said Beatrice. "This was a good choice."

"You and he were patient enough to indulge me over Iron Man. I thought this trip would make us all happy. Wine, food and scenery. I'm glad you stayed another day."

"Hmm."

"Hmm? You hate it here and want to go straight to the airport?"

"No! Certainly not. This is a lovely place and exactly the right activity to balance city sights and beaches. I was thinking that I might stay more than another day."

Will side-eyed her and nodded. "Mm-hmm."

"Don't you 'mm-hmm' me as if you know what's on my mind."

"As if indeed!" He broke into song, his bass voice soft.

"*You will never know*
And you will never care
Because you can't be there
In the mind of a woman"

Beatrice's mouth fell open in astonishment. She knew the words and the tune but had never heard them come out of Will's mouth.

"That's Apate! How on earth do you know the lyrics to a hardcore lesbian black metal song?"

"Because I was there, remember? New Year's Eve in Sweden."

"So was I but I'd never have been able to recall the words."

"We listen to that track in the car sometimes. It brings back special memories. Let's return to the point. I can't be sure what's on your mind but as a detective and old friend, I'll hazard a guess. As you told us in the car, Mia asked you to help investigate the causes of the accident in Vilanova i la Geltrú. You said no. She appealed to your better nature and you still refused. Then she floated an anomaly. An element of a mystery that doesn't add up. You've been thinking about that ever since we left Sitges and are dallying with the idea of taking the case, am I right? PI Stubbs rides again."

Beatrice ignored his accurate assessment and changed the subject. "You never told me you could sing. Does Adrian know?"

"It's a pain in the arse when someone can read your mind, isn't it? Get a move on, she's waiting to show us the cellars. Soon as that's done, we can eat."

Beatrice grinned. "*Now* you're reading my mind."

.   .   .

The most uplifting and exquisite lunch Beatrice had enjoyed in ages comprised five courses paired with exactly the right wines. Other tables in the dignified dining-room were at a sufficient distance you could almost forget they existed. Music emanated from hidden speakers, a mixture of classical guitar and piano, to cover any lapses in conversation. Not that awkward silences were a problem at Beatrice's table. From the first course of *ajoblanco* – a cold almond and garlic soup served in a dainty teacup – accompanied by an equally dainty sparkling white, Adrian's appreciation accelerated to Level 10.

Will took a sip and agreed. "Tastes like toast. No, wait, buttered toast. We should take a couple of bottles home."

"More like a case," Adrian exclaimed. "Beatrice?"

She sipped. It was a lovely fresh taste, the sort of thing Matthew would have loved. "Beautiful. The kind of wine you could have for breakfast. Did you give Montserrat a tip?"

"Of course. I also got her card in case I have questions about this year's harvest or you need tips on her lipstick. Talk about the perfectly put-together look! Spanish women have something else. I'm no expert ..."

Will caught Beatrice's eye. "Which is unlikely to stop him."

"I'm no expert, but Spanish women strut out there looking stunning, with full acknowledgement of the artifice. The French on the other hand ..."

"And for your second course, here's a helping of sweeping generalisations from someone who doesn't know what he's talking about." Will tipped up his cup and swallowed his soup. "If Catinca was here, maybe I'd give her the floor. Her job is fashion. Yours is having opinions. Do you think they'll bring us some bread?"

They brought some bread. Pan Catalan with tomatoes three ways was followed by a scoop of creamy rice with Iberian ham and cheese. Beatrice could have eaten everything on the table.

The main course, wild hake with clams and spring greens, deserved silent appreciation.

Not a bum note throughout the entire meal, unless you counted the look from the waiter when Will refused a glass of rosé in favour of a Diet Coke. The waiter flared his nostrils and suggested a sparkling water. Will caved.

Beatrice wanted to express her appreciation for these thoughtful men. "You're so very generous, Will. The car, the driving and this memorable meal. Can I take you both out for dinner tomorrow night? You mentioned an Indian place by the beach."

"So you're staying?" Adrian's face was flushed, partly by enthusiasm and partly by alcohol. "In that case, it's your turn to cook breakfast in the morning. And I don't mean a chocolate croissant from the bakery, OK? Talking of chocolate, look at what's for dessert! They have a sweet wine to go with the fifth course."

"Coffee for me," said Will. "Have you made up your mind? Stay to relax or stay to investigate? Bear in mind we're leaving on Friday."

"I haven't decided about the case. My head says it's a fool's errand because a foreigner has no hope of infiltrating a small Spanish village and cracking open its secrets. Do you remember *The Wicked Man?* That film set on a Scottish island, starring Michael Caine and Peter Cushing? A police sergeant tries to find a missing girl and ends up playing with fire."

"It was called *The Wicker Man* and the actors were Edward Woodward and Christopher Lee." Will emptied his water glass. "I'm not trying to influence you, but that movie was about pagan sacrificial rites. Village acrobatics are nowhere near the same thing. You're right though, this is out of everyone's depth, including Mia. I'd say the same as I always do – leave it to the police."

Dessert was a chocolate and bitter cherry mousse paired with a sweet wine called Nectar. Adrian and Beatrice agreed the name and label suited the refined balance and raved about the menu over coffee.

"What's the verdict?"

"We loved it all! Did we not, Beatrice?" Adrian extended his arms along the table and Beatrice knew he'd be asleep before the sun set. "Will, my love, say you liked it too or this chocolate will turn to ashes in my mouth."

"This has been an ideal day out. The whole package – scenery, fresh air, educational guide, quality food and wines I want to take home. You finish your coffee and I'll place our order." He took Adrian's rating slip from under his place mat and walked towards reception.

"That handsome beast is my husband," said Adrian, leaning against Beatrice's arm. "And I love him more than I can say."

"More than this chocolate, cherry and dessert wine combination?" asked Beatrice, scooping the last smidgen from her bowl.

"Who says I have to choose either or? Are you really going to stay with us for the rest of the week? No pressure, but please do. Will is an appalling bully and will make me hike, swim, and march around museums like a drill sergeant unless you are here to rescue me."

Beatrice rested her head on his shoulder. "I'll stay. Whether or not I can protect you from Action Man remains to be seen. My plan is to help Mia. Not sure my assistance will amount to anything, but I'll give it a shot. She wants a private investigator and there's life in this old hog yet."

"Hooray! Just make sure you solve the case by Friday, would you? Our flight leaves at two o'clock. Shall we have a brandy?"

Will appeared at Adrian's shoulder before she could reply.

"Staff members are loading our order into the car. Shall we leave now and have a nightcap at home?"

"Good idea!" shouted Beatrice, louder than was necessary. "That was a dining experience I shall never forget. Thank you, Will, and please leave the tip to me."

Will herded them outside, dragging them away from effusive thanks for every waiter and guided them to the car.

"He's pissed as a fart," laughed Beatrice as Adrian tripped over a floodlight.

"He's not the only one," Will replied. "Get in the car, both of you. Don't start singing, snoring or demanding another drink. I'll wake you up ..."

"... before you go-go," sang Adrian, sending Beatrice into fits of giggles.

Will raised his hands to the sky and said, "Give me strength."

7

The sunshine outside the station was unnecessarily bright, in Beatrice's opinion. Even after two glasses of water and an Alka-Seltzer, her head still throbbed. She put on her sunglasses, wishing she hadn't come. But here she was, sitting on a bench with Mia, waiting for the bus to Sirenes.

In cruel contrast, Mia was full of energy. "I was so pleased to get your message yesterday afternoon! It's given me a tiny sliver of hope, the first in this whole mess. I take your point about this visit being no more than establishing the facts and I agree with you. Of course, we don't know what the police have turned up, if anything, but we're far more likely to get people to talk to us. They don't know you and generally mistrust strangers on principle, but if I vouch for you, I'm hoping it will be fine. Are you all right? You're very quiet today."

"I overdid it at the winery," Beatrice confessed. "Feeling a bit fragile this morning."

"Understandable. Corpinnat sparkling wines taste dangerously innocent. My husband used to swear by Irn-Bru when he had a hangover, but that's not easy to get in Spain. Wait a moment, one of those energy drinks is bound to have a similar effect." She swept off in the direction of the kiosk. Beatrice watched her, all elegance in a navy shirt dress, her grey hair in a loose bun, silver jewellery glinting in the sun. Vaguely envious, Beatrice wondered if Catinca might be persuaded into giving her a makeover. The problem was that when it came to fashion, Catinca leaned to the radical, hence her extraordinary success. Beatrice much preferred relaxed over radical, ideally with an elastic waistband.

"Drink this but slowly. It should rebalance your blood sugar. There's the bus and thank heavens, Carlotta is behind the wheel. The younger drivers treat this route like a race track. Last week, I lost half a dozen eggs through one man's recklessness. They were free range, which made it worse." The doors opened and disgorged its passengers. Mia made no move to join the queue of people queuing to board, waiting till the driver stepped outside for a cigarette.

"Carlotta?" she murmured.

The driver, her uniform tight around her broad shoulders, looked around with a scowl. On seeing Mia, she blew out a stream of smoke and touched two fingers to her brow in a salute.

The two women conversed in Catalan, ignoring Beatrice completely. It didn't bother her; in fact she was relieved to sit quietly, sipping some highly-coloured orange drink reminiscent of Lucozade. She watched a woman across the road pause in her stroll while a Border terrier sniffed a patch of grass. Maybe she ought to go home to Huggy Bear and forget all this nonsense.

"Beatrice, we should get on. The bus leaves in five minutes. I confided in Carlotta and told her why you're here. When she's driving the bus to Sirenes, you don't have to pay."

"Hang on!" Beatrice scrambled to her feet. "I don't intend to take the bus after today. This is a one-off, I thought we agreed."

"It's a just-in-case measure. Come, let's go." Mia ushered her up the steps and into the vehicle. Carlotta started the engine with a nod to Beatrice. Around twelve people's eyes drilled into her as she walked up the aisle, ticketless and standing out like a sore thumb.

The journey took around forty minutes, during which time Beatrice's queasy headache dissipated and her clarity returned. They rumbled out of the suburbs, through farmland and villages, past an industrial estate and on cresting a hill, caught a glimpse of the sea.

Mia, who had been contentedly silent for almost half an hour, pointed out an artwork in the centre of a roundabout. "When I see them, I know I'm home. That's what Sirenes means."

Beatrice sat up to take in the sculpture as the bus drove past. Like an eternity symbol, it represented two mermaids intertwined head to tail, scales glittering, hair flowing and even though the piece was static, both figures appeared to be in constant sinuous motion. The greenish-turquoise patina lent an aquatic sheen to the piece, as if it was underwater.

"What a wonderful work of art! Do I understand that Sirenes means sirens, as in mermaids?"

"Yes, exactly. Alluring, elusive beauties attracting the unwary to their doom. The coastline of Catalonia is stunning, dramatic and wild. It's not a coincidence that so many Surrealists took their inspiration from this landscape. At the same time, it's dangerous if you don't show it respect. Look, there's the main square and the Hotel Salines, where we're meeting the mayor. We get off at this stop."

Sirenes was little more than an overgrown fishing village with a tiny harbour. Three streets ran parallel to the beach, interconnected by criss-cross of narrow lanes, populated by shops selling fishing tackle, convenience stores, cafés, *perruquerias* and an ice-cream parlour. Mia gave Beatrice the guided tour, taking in the football pitch at one end, crossing the river to the concert hall at the other, which lasted under an hour. They stopped at a stall overlooking the harbour, eating calamari and listening to the shriek of gulls.

"We do this in Devon," said Beatrice, licking her fingers. "Fish and chips by the seaside."

"And on Sundays, you have a roast dinner. I know all about a typical English country weekend. We used to do the joint of beef with all the trimmings. Even my Yorkshire pudding is passable. Are you ready? We can't keep the mayor waiting."

To Beatrice's astonishment, Mia had organised exclusive use of the hotel's library and scheduled a series of interviews with more efficiency than many of her detective sergeants at the Metropolitan Police. From two till three, the mayor of Sirenes, who was also the director of the *castello*. Next, the other two men who had formed the second level of the pyramid. Lastly, and Mia warned Beatrice he might not show up, the deceased woman's husband.

"That's quite an afternoon's work. Do I gather we won't be speaking to the man who ... erm, fainted?"

"No." Mia's expression darkened. "Bertrand Gallego isn't here. He left the village. We still don't know where he is."

The mayor was able to shed light on that question. A man of around sixty with a thatch of thick black hair and a luxurious moustache, he said he spoke no English. But he concentrated hard when Beatrice posed her questions, nodding impatiently while Mia translated. Eventually he gave up the pretence and answered immediately in Catalan.

"He says Bertrand is in Cadaqués, where his family are from. It's about two hours drive north of here."

The mayor interrupted.

"My mistake. Apparently it's more like two and a half. Bertrand left in the early hours of Sunday morning and no one knows if he's likely to return."

"I'd like to know about Bertrand's health. I assume the participants in the human towers practise for many months before Día de Sant Jordi. Did he show any signs of illness?"

The mayor seemed affronted by the question. He flared his nostrils and made definitive gesticulations as he answered. Beatrice waited as Mia said something soothing before delivering his reply in English.

"Those villagers who are chosen for the tower rehearse the year round. Sant Jordi isn't the only festival at which they perform. The mayor takes personal responsibility for everyone's fitness and safety. Last year, even after pandemic restrictions had been lifted, he insisted on masks. Anyone demonstrating any sign of less than peak fitness is replaced by one of the substitutes. Bertrand has always been one of the fittest and strongest because he is the youth football coach."

"Thank you. That's very interesting and please excuse my ignorance. Until Saturday, I had never heard of the human towers. Your commitment and collaboration is admirable. Could we talk about the day of the accident? How was Bertrand? Was there anything unusual about his behaviour?"

Mia began her translation but Beatrice could see the mayor was already thinking about the answer. His eyes drifted to the left. Beatrice could almost see him retrieving his memories while stroking his moustache. He spoke rapidly to Mia, his body language and facial expressions conveying certainty.

"He says Bertrand was a professional and would never let his emotions affect his performance. But he was under personal pressure. His property is on the far edge of town, between the football ground and the motorway. A property developer wants to buy his land to build a supermarket."

"Hypermarket," corrected the mayor. He looked at Beatrice. "*Pour la bricolage*."

She understood, although she wasn't sure why he addressed her in French. Perhaps it came more easily than English. "I see. Like a DIY store."

"Yes," agreed Mia, "like a DIY store. But Bertrand did not want to sell, even though they made three offers, each higher than the last. He refused to budge and they became threatening. He told the mayor they were trying to frighten him."

"In what way?"

The mayor shrugged, his face apologetic.

"Would you ask the mayor whether he wants a DIY store in the village?"

He didn't wait for the translation but shook his head with some vehemence, rattling off what sounded a lot like curses.

"The short answer is no," said Mia, and the man gave her a conspiratorial smile.

"As mayor, surely he has some say over planning permission?"

"No!" Again his denial was emphatic. He spoke for several minutes until ending his tirade with a hand clap.

"It's complex," answered Mia. "The land belongs to Bertrand and no formal contract exists between him and the council. It's always been an honourable agreement that Bertrand will not do anything to devalue the village. The mayor says the only chance of stopping any development would be by invoking the well. A stream flows under the property from where Bertrand draws his water. It is possible," she looked at the mayor who made a miserable moue, "but unlikely that the province might designate it a protected area. He thinks the best hope is for a long legal battle neither Bertrand nor the village of Sirenes can afford. He has another appointment now, so unless you have any more questions?"

Beatrice expressed her thanks in English and in Spanish. The mayor shook both their hands and left the library as if glad to be released.

"It's a slow process, I know," Mia apologised. "It must be very frustrating."

"It is slow, but actually rather useful. Detectives always conduct interviews in pairs, often with another pair of eyes either behind mirrored glass or more commonly these days, on video. Television dramas like to make a fuss about the good cop, bad cop scenario, but the reality is that one is the interlocutor, asking the questions while the other observes the interviewee. You'd be amazed at how much a person gives away via paralinguistic features such as eye movement, facial tics, fidgety knees and tone of voice. The mayor wasn't hiding anything, I feel sure of that, but what little he told us offers no insights. Who's next?"

Bertrand Gallego's colleagues from the second tier of the tower were eager to cooperate, which made Beatrice's heart sink. In her experience, people keen to help with an investigation were usually those with the least to offer. But these two explained the mechanics of how the tower was constructed and Beatrice was enthralled. The attention to detail was extraordinary, from the tying of the sash to establishing a foothold to the arm lock each man used to grip his fellows. As to why Bertrand had collapsed, neither man could enlighten them.

Mia translated their words but Beatrice had already seen the incomprehension and puzzlement on their faces. "He doesn't drink, he's healthier than most thirty-year-olds, he trains the young footballers and he's been part of the *castello* team since he was a teenager. They hope doctors at the hospital can explain more when the police release that information."

They did the handshaking, expressing sorrow, thanking them for their time and said goodbye. But the two men hesitated and asked Mia something Beatrice didn't understand.

"I'm just going to step outside for a moment. Probably some personal stuff." Mia gave her a reassuring smile.

Beatrice nodded her assent and stood up to stretch her legs. The windows of the library faced away from the sea with a view of a church against a hillside beyond. It really was a delightful village yet somehow draped with sadness since the events of the weekend. She wished she could have seen it before Saturday's tragedy.

The door opened and Mia returned with a younger man, his face shadowed and somehow devoid of hope, like a prisoner jailed for life.

"Beatrice, this is Joan Soler, husband of Núria. Joan, this is my friend Beatrice. We can speak in English as Joan is a translator."

"Good afternoon, Joan. I am deeply sorry for your loss. Thank you for coming to talk to me at such a difficult time." She stretched out a hand and he took it, his grip strong.

"Thank you, but I have nothing to tell you. I wasn't even there. My son and I stayed home. Mia, I don't want to seem ungrateful, but I'm telling you this is a waste of time. It was a horrible, unfortunate accident and no amount of enquiries or investigations can bring Núria back."

Such a non sequitur was hard to follow. Mia looked nonplussed and close to tears.

Beatrice dispensed with platitudes and adopted a hard-edged professional tone. "That much is true. Nevertheless, an understanding of the circumstances surrounding your wife's death might contribute to the healing process for everyone involved. It's only natural that your grief is a black spot obliterating your vision. The entire village feels your pain, I sensed it the moment we got off the bus, and if your neighbours could carry one share of your suffering, they would."

He didn't reply, his eyes downcast.

"In that spirit, are you willing to answer a few questions? It won't take long." She gestured to the chair but he shook his head.

"I'll stand. What do you want to know?"

"Why did you and your son stay home rather than watching your village take part in Día de Sant Jordi?"

His eyes flashed and Beatrice knew she'd hit a nerve.

"We grounded our son. He got into trouble and we wanted him to learn a lesson. No *festas* for a week, Núria and I agreed. Raimon is seventeen and headstrong. He wouldn't stay home unless one of us was there to watch him. It was Núria's turn to take part in the *castello* and that's why I volunteered to stay with Raimon. We first heard what happened on social media."

Every sentence he uttered exacerbated his pain. Beatrice couldn't bear to see the man suffer any further, but she had one last link to explore.

"Does Raimon play football?"

Joan glanced at her, a flicker of surprise in his eyes. "Yes. He's the goalie for the under-eighteens. Or he was, until Bertrand sacked him."

"Why would Bertrand sack your son?"

"He caught Raimon smoking weed and dropped him from the squad. That was Thursday. He came to the house to explain and we supported his decision. Raimon wants to be a sportsman. How the hell does he expect to make it when his head is fuzzy with marijuana? Núria and I were united. Actions have consequences. Raimon was sacked from the team and grounded until he'd learned his lesson."

"Thursday. So Raimon didn't leave your house at all before Saturday?"

"No. On Friday morning, he got out of the attic window and onto the roof. Núria spotted him and phoned me at work. He did it on purpose. There was no way he could get down but he knew his mother wouldn't follow him onto the roof because she suffers from vertigo. It was a stunt, a threat to scare us. It didn't work. We locked him in his room."

Beatrice glanced from him to Mia. "Núria suffered from vertigo? Why would anyone with such a condition volunteer to climb a human pyramid?"

With a grunt, Joan shoved the chair forwards until it hit the desk. He walked to the door without looking back. As he passed Mia, he spat out a sentence in English, his voice low and contemptuous.

"She was the best you could do?" He wrenched the door open and stalked out, leaving it swinging behind him.

Mia pressed her hands to her eyes. "My fault. I should have given you a full explanation. Núria Soler didn't fall from the tower. She wasn't even in the pyramid, but part of the support team or safety net. When the tower collapsed, falling bodies crushed her to death."

Beatrice bowed her head and closed her eyes.

The long miserable journey to Vilanova i la Geltrú was made worse by three factors. First, Carlotta wasn't driving and the lunatic behind the wheel clearly had a death wish. Second, darkness scrubbed any hope of seeing attractive scenery. All she could see was the reflection of a teenager wearing trainers the size of breeze blocks bobbing his head to some tinny sounds coming from his earphones. Third, she was alone. Mia had remained in Sirenes, promising to talk to anyone else who had been present at the accident.

Beatrice huffed through her nostrils. A total and utter waste of time. Factor four, she was hungry. She sent Adrian a message.

On my way back to Sitges, arriving around 9pm. Is that too late for a curry? Bx

She stared out of the window, mentally assembling her perfect menu. Onion bhajis, a dhal with spinach, naan bread and something chunky like paneer masala. No wine after yesterday, but a Kingfisher beer would do nicely. Her phone vibrated.

Sorry, we've already eaten. Hungry hippos with hangovers couldn't wait. Want me to meet you at the station? Ax

She left it a few minutes to suppress her petulance.

No need, but thanks for offering. Save me some dry bread and gruel. Bx

8

The moment Beatrice awoke on Tuesday morning, part of yesterday's conversation repeated itself in her head.

'Bertrand did not want to sell, even though they made three offers, each higher than the last. He refused to budge and they became threatening. He told the mayor they were trying to frighten him.'

After her shower, she sent Mia a message asking for the name of the hypermarket which sought to buy Bertrand's land. Then she went in search of breakfast. Last night, Adrian had been kind enough to prepare her a Croque Monsieur but that was hardly enough to keep body and soul together. No one was in the kitchen and the boys' bedroom door was open. They must have set off early for that hike Will was banging on about. The kitchen table was set for one and a note propped against a coffee cup.

Will's gone off up some mountain and I've lost my Radu jacket. Going to the pizzeria to see if I left it there. Returning via the bakery, natch. If you need anything else, call. Ax

She rustled through the fridge and assembled the ingredients for a mushroom and herb omelette, made coffee and read Mia's reply.

The name of the hypermarket is El Castor. *The person negotiating with Bertrand on their behalf is a property lawyer from Tarragona. Waiting for confirmation of the firm's name. Do I understand you're taking the case? If so, we need to discuss your fee.*

Beatrice ate her omelette, considering what to say. She still hadn't formulated a response when Adrian burst in with his Radu jacket, a bag of pastries and a huge smile. "Paris!"

"No, I'm Beatrice. You found it then?"

"What? Yes, the owner kept it for me, but never mind that! We're going to Paris!"

"We are?"

"You've been up long enough to make yourself breakfast but haven't checked your emails? Sometimes I worry about you. Catinca has invited us to her first ever fashion show in Paris! Front row at a Radu show, Beatrice! We'll be rubbing shoulders with A-listers, featured in gossip zines and get plastered all over Instagram. You can practise your French skills and I can prance up and down the Champs Elysees in outfits to die for. The tragedy is I have absolutely nothing to wear."

Beatrice relieved him of the bag of pastries. "Mmm, pain au chocolat. Can I have this?"

"Have it all, I'm not going to eat anything other than miso soup for the next fortnight. One minute I'm thinking colour, the next I want to go full on winter dramatics. Will couldn't care less and Catinca won't mind, but I want to sit there like Anna Wintour. A magnet for the paparazzi."

"What do you mean by a fortnight? When is this fashion show?"

"A week on Saturday!" Adrian crossed his eyes, scrolled through his phone and showed Beatrice the invitation. It did look sophisticated and rather posh, not at all Beatrice's kind of thing. However, Paris held some special memories for herself and for Catinca. And she had to admit she was curious to try out her ability in French.

"That brilliant young woman. How fabulous! I am thrilled to be invited and wouldn't miss this for the world. Good Lord, it's not even two weeks from now! I'll barely have time to unpack before dashing off again. I'm turning into a jet-setter, at my age. We can get the Eurostar from London, can't we?"

Adrian crossed his arms across his chest and closed his eyes. Apart from the pink in his cheeks, he might have been embalmed.

"What?"

He opened his eyes. "What? Exactly the right question. WHAT am I going to wear?"

As so many mornings before, Beatrice and Adrian grazed, chatted and relaxed in each other's company. He showed her images of what he considered hot looks in male fashion; she wrinkled her nose. She polished off a flaky twist filled with nuts while he ate three croissants. When she checked her phone, there was good news. Mia had found the law firm: Suarez y Chan, Tarragona.

"Do you have plans for the day?" asked Beatrice, as she rinsed the dishes.

"Other than checking every trend in male couture from here to New York? Nothing. Why, where do you want to go and what for?"

"I thought I'd like to see a bit more of the region. Tarragona is only an hour away."

"Are there shops?"

"And restaurants. Shall we?"

Adrian folded his arms and gave her a searching look. "Why Tarragona? Tell me the truth."

"I want to visit a law firm. It might be pertinent to the case."

"Do you have an appointment with this law firm?"

Beatrice frowned. "How am I supposed to make an appointment without speaking any Spanish?"

"How are you supposed to get any information from them if you can't get in? Sit down and tell me the background. When we have worked out our story, we'll call Manu and see if he can't wangle us an audience. He's the kindest and most helpful man I ever met and I feel an absolute fool for suspecting him."

"Suspecting him of what?"

"Preying on Will."

"Why on earth would you think he was preying on Will?"

Adrian lifted his shoulders and opened his palms as if the answer was obvious. "Because that's exactly what I would do if I saw a hot man who needed help. Opportunism, Beatrice, is my middle name. Now, about this law firm."

Mr Adrian Harvey, wine merchant, restauranteur and European businessman was looking to expand his empire. Impressed with the quality of Catalonian cuisine and viniculture, he sought a suitable location to found a wine warehouse with the intention of establishing an import/export business. His financial adviser, Ms Stubbs, accompanied him to all site visits and business meetings to take accurate notes. He had been advised that the villages of Calafell and Sirenes had potential, due to excellent transport connections. The next step was to hire a lawyer to assist with the acquisition process. Suarez y Chan came highly recommended.

Manu called back to confirm he had squeezed in a half-hour appointment with one of the English-speaking partners at 15.00.

"Isn't he a darling? He didn't even ask why we need to see a lawyer. Right, do we have our story straight, PI Stubbs?"

"Yes!" Beatrice enthused. "You talk and I listen. It always

works better that way. So long as you stick to the script. On the train, we will devise a series of questions. You may not ad lib nor improvise, is that understood?"

Adrian gave her his Princess Diana look from under his lashes.

"Secondly, I can't use the name Stubbs, just in case they go digging. Your profile on the Internet is exactly what you say. But far too much investigative work attached to the name Stubbs for comfort. Why don't you refer to me as Mrs Brown?"

"Mrs Brown? Who wrote this script? We'll call you Ms Quinn, which is a very good name for a detective. Go and raid your wardrobe for business-woman type of attire. Ooh, I am looking forward to this! It's taken my mind right off the wardrobe crisis. Get a shift on and we can get the next train, have lunch and arrive at our meeting exactly on time."

Business-woman kind of attire meant one thing – her trusty grey suit. There was no better way to fade into the background. She wore no jewellery, left her scarves in the wardrobe, brushed on a touch of mascara and stepped onto the platform at Tarragona station looking eminently forgettable. Her focus on the upcoming interview, Beatrice was uninterested in sight-seeing. Nevertheless, since they had two hours till their rendezvous, she indulged Adrian with a visit to the Roman amphitheatre beside the sea. How the audience could keep their eyes on the action while the ocean whispered and shim-mered at their backs was anyone's guess. The place was imbued with an expectancy and respect, so that one could almost visualise those long-dead performers stepping into their roles.

When Adrian proposed a short walk to the ancient chariot race circuit, she accepted with alacrity. "Let's go! How come

Tarragona has so many Roman sites? Is it me or can you actually feel the city's history through your shoes?"

"I adore Roman architecture," Adrian breathed. "Can you imagine how jaw-dropping this was in its heyday? Chariots pounding around this arena and roaring crowds cheering them on. Thrilling! I would have made a wonderful Roman because I've got the legs for a toga."

Beatrice glanced at his shorts. "You do have good legs. As for a Roman, I'm not sure. They were awfully bloody, you know."

"Oh, I know. No gladiator role for me. I'm talking Emperor-level with a male harem and a personal chef. On that note, what do you say about lunch?"

Beatrice snorted. "Something tells me you didn't pass your history exams. Where are we eating? You gave me so many options while we were on the train, they all blended into one."

"I picked a place one street away from the law firm offices. It has rave reviews, offers a menu of the day with three courses and its wine cellar is legendary. I reserved us an outside table, seeing as the weather is lovely. Then a casual stroll to meet Ona Suarez and a train ride along the coast. I could see myself living here. Would you come and visit?"

Beatrice slipped her arm into the crook of his elbow. "As you well know, I would visit you and Will wherever you settled. Have you memorised your questions? We should run through it again over lunch. One other thing, we can't drink too much wine. We're at work."

"Trust me, Beatrice, I'm a professional. There it is! The one with the striped awnings."

Telling Adrian not to drink too much wine was like telling a dog not to pee on a tree. They ate a silky smooth dish of scallops in brown butter with green beans, drank an effervescent white

Penedès and rehearsed their pitch. Adrian was already in character which Beatrice found faintly ludicrous seeing as he was playing himself. She had to shush him several times as he pontificated over coffee.

She paid the bill and they turned up outside the building housing the law firm a few minutes before three. It was situated above a bank, a discreet little door plate the only indication of which business operated there. With one last intense glare at her sidekick, Beatrice pressed the bell.

"*Sí?*"

Adrian cleared his throat and inhaled as if embarking on a soliloquy from Hamlet. "Good afternoon. My name is Adrian Harvey of Harvey's Wine Emporium and I am accompanied by my financial adviser, Ms Quinn. We have an appointment at three o'clock. Please inform Señora Suarez her guests are here."

The door buzzed and Adrian shoved it open. "After you, Ms Quinn."

Beatrice shot him an admiring look. "Do you know, I think you would have made a very good Roman indeed."

The offices were faux impressive, with cork floors and large armchairs around glass coffee tables strewn with pretentious magazines. Adrian strode ahead to reception only to be intercepted by a short woman with eyebrows the size of caterpillars.

"Mr Harvey? Ona Suarez. Come this way." Her eyes skated over Beatrice. "Can I get you something to drink?"

"Water, please. Still. My assistant would like to record this meeting, if that's all right?"

"No. Sorry. Legal meetings are private affairs. This is the conference room. You sit there and she can sit next to you."

Who's she? The cat's mother? Beatrice maintained her composure but gritted her teeth.

Adrian delivered his spiel with typical flair, during which time the Suarez woman fixed him with a severe glare.

"How did you get my name?"

"Oh, I didn't. During a business lunch last week, someone recommended your firm as specialist in land acquisition." He looked at Beatrice. "Do you remember who it was?"

"I think it might have been that supermarket chap. I can't recall his name."

"Do you mean Juan Ferrera of El Castor?" asked Suarez.

"El Castor!" echoed Beatrice, her glee at the woman's gullibility adding a tone of genuine excitement. "That was it. I remember because we saw one of his stores on the way out of Barcelona."

"Yes. I am representing El Castor's interests in a business deal."

"He spoke very highly of your company," said Adrian. "When we told him Sirenes was top on our list of prospective locations, he suggested we get in touch."

"Sirenes is rather small for a wine business. It's getting busier now but during the winter season, it all but closes down. I would say somewhere like Vilanova or Sitges would be a better choice. There's a lot more activity in those places."

"If we were talking about a public-facing direct outlet, I would agree with you. However, this is a wholesale operation, for trade professionals. We buy selected high-end local and international wines and export them to wine shops and restaurants across Europe. The store would be open to vintners, chefs, sommeliers and hotel representatives where they can taste or get advice on what stock to purchase for the coming year. I have investors and a client list all lined up."

Beatrice nodded solemnly.

Adrian continued, his manner imperious. "All I need is the right location. It must be accessible from the motorway and somewhere between Barcelona and Tarragona. Sirenes looks perfect. The supermarket fellow said he's building a new store there and I sense the place might become more attractive to other businesses. Therefore, the prices will rise. I want to get in now, while land is still affordable."

Suarez's eyes glittered. "I take your point. In fact, there is a tract of very affordable land about to become available. El Castor wants two thousand square metres for a DIY store, but there would be plenty left over. We're currently negotiating a price with the owner. Would you like to see it? Then we could take you on as a client and acquire the land on your behalf."

"That sounds like a very good plan. Shall we go, Ms Quinn?"

Beatrice was already on her feet. The half-hour meeting was more elastic than it seemed.

Suarez drove a Hyundai Tucson and took the opportunity of a forty-minute drive to test Adrian's story. Beatrice sat in the back seat, totally ignored and painfully tense in case Adrian went off script and blew their cover. She needn't have worried. Ona Suarez was only interested in one thing – money. She quizzed Adrian on his background, his existing ventures, the business model for the wine warehouse and probed as far as she dared in terms of what he was willing to spend. She was wearing sunglasses, unfortunately, but Beatrice could swear she saw dollar signs in her eyes.

They drove past the mermaids sculpture and instead of heading into the centre of the village, took a left towards the football ground. Suarez parked at the far end and indicated the development area with a sweep of her arm.

"From here up to the motorway bridge and all the way across to the creek. As it stands, there's a chance we can acquire the football ground as part of the package. When the townspeople find out they're sitting on a goldmine used by nobody else but a few teenagers, I think they'll be ready to sell."

Adrian strode around the perimeter, asking questions and making observations. Beatrice stayed put, sitting on a bench provided for the football supporters. Across the other side of the pitch she made out a track leading to a property half hidden by ancient stubby trees. Bertrand's home, she assumed. She pulled out her phone and dialled Adrian's number.

"Hello?"

"Hello, Mr Harvey and I'm sorry to disturb you. This is a very important business acquaintance of yours calling to ask for your decision on some multi-squillion dollar deal. Say lots of big financial words and do the whole Wolf of Wall Street thing, then hang up and keep that woman occupied down that end of the field while I poke about. Understood?"

There was a pause at the end of the line. "Jordan, what do I pay you for? This is not a rhetorical question. I believe my instructions were perfectly comprehensible. The 2019 Bordeaux harvest is worth far more than what they're asking. We are not haggling over a Turkish carpet here, but stealing a march on a raft of sublime wines which will form the bedrock of my new enterprise. On that note, I'm with an agent surveying a potential location as we speak. I gave you my authority to purchase the château's entire range at full price. One would expect a discount, naturally, but quality comes with a cost and I'm prepared to pay it. The next time I answer a call from you, I expect a done deal. Have a productive afternoon." The phone went dead.

Jordan? Where on earth had he got that from? Beatrice wandered about the football field, projecting the image of a woman at a loose end until she was sure she was out of sight. Then she made a beeline for the house behind the hedge. It looked as if it had been there for centuries. A strip of rough grass and weeds was flanked by two dusty vehicle tracks. The garden was well tended and practical with vegetable patches and a herb garden among the flowers. Beatrice approached, balancing confidence and caution in case there was a dog on guard. But the place appeared deserted with no more life than the bees populating the lavender plants.

She walked up to the front door and knocked three times. There was a veranda stretching around three quarters of the building, with a view down to the sea. A wrought iron bench scattered with faded cushions in one corner faced the beach, a table of similar design to its right. This was evidently a place for one person. Beatrice could envisage the owner with his legs up, his back supported and a strong coffee beside him on the table. On the porch, she saw how this man's life was shaped by two views: the sea and the football field. She understood and a little part of her envied Bertrand Gallego.

Since there was no answer at the door, she walked around the house to get a sense of proportion, peering into the windows when the opportunity arose. The place was relatively large, with two storeys, green shutters and terracotta pots of more herbs outside the kitchen. A sandy path led from the back door to a small shed, which Beatrice initially dismissed until she recalled the mayor's mention of a well. The door was on a simple latch. She opened it and looked inside, her eyes taking a moment to adjust. In the centre stood a stone circle, its cemented rocks reaching to around hip height, covered by a wooden lid not dissimilar to the end of a barrel. Beatrice stayed in the doorway, wary of spiders. Beside the well lay a chain with a hook and a bucket.

She considered trying to open the well but the sound of voices made her retreat. Adrian and Ona Suarez walked across the football field, her laugh carrying across the afternoon air. Not wanting to be caught trespassing, Beatrice scuttled around the hedge and caught up with them as they returned to the car.

"Ah, there you are. We had a thorough look around and I

think this place has definite potential. What are your thoughts, Ms Quinn?"

"I see a great many variables, Mr Harvey. Electricity and water supplies, for example, in addition to a serious concern regarding accessibility from the main road. Not only that, but there seems to be an inhabited property the other side of the football field. All things considered, I would say this is the least developed site we've seen so far and therefore will require the most investment."

Adrian stroked his chin. "Someone is living here?" He turned to Suarez. "I understood this was a vacant lot."

"It is, it most certainly is. The old man who used to live there left the village in disgrace. It's a sad story, but not unusual, I'm afraid. An elderly bachelor living alone, drinking too much and with an unhealthy interest in young boys. The people of the town tried to help him but as we say, trash floats to the top. His indiscipline caused a fatal accident at a local festival last weekend. They've driven him out and he won't be returning. We expect his signature on the contract any day now. To be honest, he should pay us for saving his reputation. Ms Quinn, I commissioned a full surveyor's report on this land. If Mr Harvey wishes to proceed, I am prepared to share that with you. That will allay all your fears regarding infrastructure." She looked at her watch. "It's almost six and it will soon be dark. Can I invite you for a glass of sherry to discuss this prospect further?"

Beatrice jumped in before Adrian could open his mouth. "Unfortunately not. Mr Harvey has an engagement later this evening. Would you mind driving us to Vilanova i la Geltrú so we can catch a train back to Barcelona?"

Suarez gave Beatrice an acidic look. "It would be a pleasure. Mr Harvey, let me give you my card. Why don't we talk tomorrow to take the next steps in securing this highly desirable piece of land?"

With a stroke of brilliant timing, Adrian's phone rang. He answered, adopting the impatient tone he had used with 'Jordan'.

"Hello? Ah yes, thanks for returning my call, Mr Fox. I can confirm that my assistant and I will be joining you at the restaurant this evening as agreed. I'm in a meeting right now, but I look forward to seeing you at dinner. Goodbye."

Beatrice would have given anything to see Will's face.

9

Poor Will. All he wanted to do after his physical challenge was relax and enjoy a week of beautiful scenery, good food, entertaining company, involving absolutely no detective work. Beatrice sympathised with his predicament but she had a sneaking suspicion that after hearing of today's findings, curiosity would persuade him into a busman's holiday. In any case, she needed his insight.

Cards on the table, she decided, and invited Mia to join them at the Indian restaurant. Knowledge was subject to interpretation. It might reveal its secrets under scrutiny or collapse under the bright light of an analytical mind.

At least Mia showed positive interest in where Will had been hiking and asked perceptive questions. It helped. His lack of enthusiasm when it came to private investigation was due to an establishment mindset. In Will's view, and Beatrice generally agreed, anything resembling a serious crime should be handled by the police. Where they disagreed was on how to get the police interested in the first place. On this occasion, the balance worked in Beatrice's favour. Mia was deeply invested in this case as she had known both victim and alleged cause of death. Beatrice had been present at the event and she was therefore personally committed to rooting out the truth. Adrian had given an extraordinary performance and gained a trove of information. Faced with passion, commitment and giddy enthusiasm, poor Will didn't stand a chance.

The other factor driving Beatrice was her appetite. When one mentally plans an Indian meal and is thwarted, the next chance must be grabbed with both hands. For starters, they ordered bhajis, pakoras, poppadums and chickpea croquettes to share. Beatrice gave Mia the floor.

She made an excellent witness. She began at the beginning, gave a reasonable amount of context, painted the characters with a touch of colour and conveyed the true horror of what happened on Saturday with a few well chosen words and a genuinely pained expression.

Will had questions but Beatrice forestalled him until she and Adrian had delivered their own report. She let Adrian go first because the chickpea croquettes absorbed the majority of her attention.

"Yes, well, the portrait you just painted of Bertrand Gallego is quite different to the image Ona Suarez described. Correct me if I'm wrong, Beatrice, but she said the owner of the property behind the football field was a single man with a drinking problem whom the villagers suspected of paedophilia. After his drunken exhibition at the festival, the people chased him out of town."

Beatrice shot Will a glance. "I think this is a classic example of witness interpretation. You're not wrong, Adrian, but it's important we report exactly what she said, not what she wanted us to think. Ona Suarez described him as an elderly bachelor living alone. She didn't use the word alcoholic but she did say he drank to excess. As for the reference to paedophilia, she called it 'an unhealthy interest in young boys'. At no point did she say where that information came from or whether it was her own supposition merely because he coached the junior football team. Had we been in an interview room, I would have pressed her on the point. She painted a picture of a man at odds with his community and actually used the words 'they drove him out'. She expressed full confidence in the fact that he was unlikely to return and on the cusp of signing his land away. It was casually delivered but still hyperbole. She wanted to twist the truth to suit us. Mia?"

The older woman pressed her hands to her face, shaking her head.

"Are you all right?" asked Will, handing her a napkin to dry her tears.

But there were no tears to dry. When Mia released her hands and met their gaze, her eyes were blazing with fury.

"Everything she said is a filthy lie! Everything! Bertrand is a valued member of the village, probably second to the mayor in terms of the respect that he commands. No one ran him out of town, he left in the middle of the night and everyone was distraught by his departure. Elderly? He's fifty-two years old and fitter than most thirty-year-olds, as Beatrice heard from his colleagues in the *castello*. He lives alone, that much is true, but that's because he's a widower. His wife worked on the lifeboats and lost her life trying to save others. You could walk around Sirenes, asking anyone about Bertrand Gallego, and they will tell you two things: he's crazy about football and he doesn't drink. That foul woman should be ashamed of herself, telling such scurrilous untruths."

Her passion stunned the table into silence.

Will was the first to speak. "May I offer a detective inspector's impressions? Work with me here, Beatrice. If this case landed on your desk at the Met, what would be your first plan of action? Let's start with the incident in Vilanova with the collapsing pyramid."

"If I were in an official position with authority," Beatrice put down her croquette and concentrated, "I would speak to the hospital staff who treated the victim and the man who collapsed. I would ask for toxicology reports and as soon as possible, interview the individual personally. None of those options are open to me as a private investigator. Instead I have familiarised myself with the background and spoken to several of the people involved."

Will was unimpressed. "You mean you've listened to gossip. All I'm hearing is second or even third-hand suppositions. As you just told Adrian, you have to listen between the lines. The property developer certainly sounds like a shit-stirring trouble-maker out for her own ends, but that doesn't necessarily incriminate her in any wrongdoing. When you say none of those options are open to you, I'm afraid I disagree. You haven't spoken to Bertrand Gallego, the man at the centre all of this story, which seems the obvious place to start. Are we done with the starters?" He flicked his eyes at the hovering waiter.

"Certainly not. Let's put them all on one plate to make room for the main courses."

They reorganised the table and allowed the waiter to set their meals on elegant dish warmers. No one spoke, merely smiling and nodding as the food arrived. It smelt delicious and Beatrice could not wait to tuck in, but she also needed time to think.

Her half-hearted attempts at establishing facts were indeed little more than listening to gossip. At the crux of the issue was her reluctance to take on the job. She wanted a few more days of sunshine, companionship and chickpea croquettes, no emotional engagement with other people's tragedies, and enough time to do her washing before she left for Paris. Much as she liked Mia, this was a job for the police.

"Even if you could speak to the police, they wouldn't give much away," said Mia, spooning some okra onto her plate. "The police inspector in Villanova is the opposite of dynamic. She moves at her own pace, which is so slow that by the time she gets results, everyone has forgotten what the crime was. On the other hand, I think Bertrand would talk to you. It would mean a two-hour drive along the coast, almost to the border with France, but it is beautiful scenery and you could hear the story from the horse's mouth."

"You know where he is, Mia?" asked Will.

She nibbled on some naan bread. "I think I do. The mayor mentioned Bertrand had returned to the town where he grew up. Both parents are dead and his only remaining relative is his sister, who still lives in Cadaqués."

"Cadaqués!" Adrian put down his fork and boggled his eyes at Will. "Oh my God, I don't believe it! This was meant to be. For me, the single most attractive place of my dreams in Catalonia was Cadaqués. And Figueres. We could drive there tomorrow, take Mia and Beatrice and pay homage to my all-time hero, Salvador Dalí. Please, Will, my love, my darling, my angel, can we please go to Cadaqués?"

With all three pair of eyes on him, Will sighed. "The single most attractive place of your dreams in Catalonia, apart from Barcelona, Sitges and the Corpinnat winery, is actually *two* other places you've never previously mentioned in your life?"

"It's an artist's colony famed for bohemian surrealists." Adrian clasped his hands under his chin and made doe eyes at his husband. "It calls to my creative soul."

Will laughed, his head lifted to the ceiling. "You are the

worst. OK, I'll hire a car and drive us all to whatever it's called. Now can we eat?"

The drive to Figueres was smooth along well-maintained motorways with impressive views. Beatrice sat in the passenger seat beside Will, assisting as navigator. In the rear, Mia and Adrian chatted easily about all kind of subjects, becoming firm friends over the course of the journey. He complimented her stylish dusty-pink jumpsuit accessorised with a dove-grey shrug. In response, she admired his jacket.

"The cut suits you as if it was tailor-made."

"No, it is a designer piece but off the peg. The other night I almost lost it by leaving it in a pizza restaurant! Can you imagine? An original Radu?"

"That's an original Radu? I adore her clothes. I'm saving up for one of her coats this winter."

Will interrupted. "We're approaching Figueres. Shall we stop for lunch here or press on to Cadaqués? I'm about ready for a break."

"Lunch!" squeaked Beatrice.

Adrian moaned. "I am absolutely starving!"

"I know just the place," added Mia. "And I'm paying because I've travelled here many times before but never with such an excellent driver."

Will grinned. "Figueres it is."

The dynamic changed into professionalism over lunch. Beatrice and Will prepared questions for Bertrand, with Mia's guidance. As a local, Mia knew the man and the circumstances. As detectives, Beatrice and Will knew the protocol. Between them, they worked out how to extract the information they needed. Adrian offered to assist, eager to play his part, but Beatrice understood the delicacy of such a conversation.

There was no guarantee Bertrand would even give them an audience.

"Far better that you and Will soak up the scenery and leave us to talk to this beleaguered man. There's every chance he'll reject me or both of us. At least you should make the most of the journey north. Two days left of our holiday and hasn't it gone so fast?"

Her comment deflated all three of her companions and Beatrice regretted her choice of words.

"Still, Manchego and tomatoes make for a jolly good combination. Anyone for a top up?"

The winding road over the mountain kept them all awake and the descent to Cadaqués was enough to wake the sleepiest passenger.

"Look at the sea!" Adrian gasped. "That colour simply cannot be real! Will, now can you understand why I was determined to come here?"

"I can. It's breathtaking. There must be some geological explanation for this quality of light. It's inspirational. No wonder it attracted so many artists."

Beatrice stared. "How come no one ever told me about this place?"

"The locals want to keep it as it is," replied Mia. "They don't advertise and generally discourage tourists. I can't say I blame them."

The two women wished the men a pleasant afternoon, then climbed a steep hill behind the church which dominated the charming town. Pretty villas with abundant foliage lined the lane where Bertrand's sister lived. When they found her house, the gate was wide open but Mia suggested ringing the bell beside the post box out of politeness. There was no reply. They looked at each other, wondering what to do next. Two steps inside the gate, Beatrice spotted a deckchair behind an orange tree, with a pair of trousered legs clearly visible. They made their way along the path and found a man dozing with a black cat on his lap, a discarded newspaper and a cup of coffee on the ground beside him. The scene reminded Beatrice so forcefully of Matthew she stopped to catch her breath.

The cat looked up as Mia approached, its green eyes unblinking. The man's face was shadowed by the brim of his straw hat, so Beatrice couldn't see his eyes.

"Bertrand?" Mia ventured, her voice gentle.

He turned his head to see who had spoken and all echoes of Matthew disappeared. This man was stocky and tanned, with a rough beard and wiry black hair just starting to grey. He sat up and the cat slithered off, slinking into the bushes.

"Mia?" He voice showed disbelief, as if he might still be dreaming.

"*Olà*, Bertrand." She made a hurried speech in Catalan. Beatrice stayed where she was until Mia mentioned her name, then stepped forward with a smile. Bertrand nodded his acknowledgement of her existence but didn't seem particularly pleased to see her. He muttered something guttural, got up and walked towards the house.

"He says there's nothing to tell, but seeing as we've come all this way, the least he can do is offer us a glass of lemonade."

They followed him along a path like those she'd seen in Barcelona, made from pieces of broken tiles. It was colourful and random, similar to the garden itself which was overflowing with colour and scent. By the back door stood a heavy table, its surface a ceramic pattern of citrus fruits, surrounded by four folding chairs. Bertrand set down a jug of cloudy liquid and three chunky tumblers. He said something to Beatrice which she didn't understand. On seeing her blank expression, he jerked a chin at Mia.

"He says his English is rusty but asks if you understand French."

Beatrice opened her mouth to reply in the negative but saw she was about to miss an opportunity. "If you can help me when I get stuck and he speaks slowly, yes, we can have this conversation in French." She nodded at Bertrand. "*Oui, je comprends le français.*"

He poured the lemonade, informed her his sister made it and asked her opinion of Cadaqués. Haltingly at first and fearful of making a mistake, she offered her admiration of the town, pleased she remembered the word '*incroyable*'.

He agreed, gave a sad smile as he surveyed the terracotta roofs and shimmering sea, and said, "It's beautiful like nowhere else on earth. But my heart belongs to Sirenes."

A sigh dragged from the depths escaped him and Beatrice saw all the signs of a broken heart. Shadows under his eyes spoke of sleepless nights, hunched shoulders signalled defeat and even here, in a garden with a view to make anyone rejoice, he carried an air of bleak despair.

Mia's voice, soft and reassuring, spoke in clear, classic French. "As I told you, Beatrice is an investigator. She works for herself and has no affiliation with the police. We have spoken to the mayor and two of your colleagues, along with Joan Soler."

Bertrand winced at the name as if he had toothache.

"Everyone agrees what happened that day was not normal. No one blames you but there is a desire to get at the truth. I haven't even told Beatrice yet, but the town council have offered to pay for her services. They refuse to accept the explanation that you were drunk and passed out."

Bertrand remained silent, running two fingers over the grooves in his forehead.

"We learned a property lawyer wanted to acquire your land for an El Castor outlet. Beatrice went to Tarragona and the offices of Suarez y Chan, met Ona Suarez and heard her version of your circumstances. *Connerie, quelle connerie!*"

That word was a new one to Beatrice and she glanced at Mia for clarification. "Bullshit," she explained.

"*Ce n'est pas une surprise*," said Bertrand, half under his breath.

"We came here today to ask you for your version of events. I appreciate we may be able to achieve nothing at all, but our aim is to get to the truth. Will you help us? Please, Bertrand, all we want is to clear your name."

He shook his head. "You can't clear my name, Mia. My failure hurt the whole village and cost Núria Soler her life. That is a fact."

"But you don't drink alcohol!" Beatrice interjected. "The doctor found alcohol in your blood? Why?"

His shoulders almost touched his ears and he opened his palms. "*Aucune idée.*"

Beatrice exchanged a glance with Mia. If he had no idea, who did? The man gave the very strong impression he had given up and resigned himself to taking the blame, deserved or otherwise. Somehow, they had to light a flame under this man and ignite the urge to fight.

"Suarez took us to your land. El Castor wants most of it but she's prepared to sell the rest to smaller enterprises. She said it's a waste of space as only a few teenagers use the football field."

Her barb hit its target. His eyes flashed. "Ours is the best kept field in amateur football along the whole coast! Why else would the under-eighteens league hold the championship there? Suarez is a liar and a cheat."

"When did she make her first offer? I assume it was her and not her partner, Mr Chan."

"Chan doesn't exist. She says she has a business partner in Shanghai but no one has ever seen him. It's just a way of making herself look international and appeal to Chinese investors. The business belongs to Suarez. She buys land, chops it into lots and sells them to the highest bidder. I've heard stories about her. People say she will go to any lengths. She hires troublemakers to make residents uncomfortable or deliberately pollutes the water supply so surveyors undervalue the selling price. She is ruthless and the last time I spoke to her, I told her to go to hell."

"When was that?" Without even realising she'd done it, Beatrice had taken out her notebook and was writing down key facts.

"Four days before Día de St Jordi . Some young men turned up at the café where the junior team hang out. It's a decent place where they expect good behaviour. The owner called me and said some of my teens were smoking drugs outside. I ran over there, caught them in the act and suspended all three from the team. The owner promised to call me next time any pushers came sniffing around so I could give them a warning. Suarez was waiting at my place when I got home. That's how I know she's behind this. I can't prove it, but that's what she does, spoils everything and when everyone leaves, she cleans up."

"What did she say to you?"

Bertrand clenched his fists and his jaw. "She offered me more money to sell the land. According to her, it was my last chance to 'do things nicely'. I dislike swearing and violence but I told her to you-know-what herself and if she ever set foot on my property again, I would throw her down the well. I regret being so rude. Then again, there's only so much I can tolerate."

"I agree. I wanted to curse the horrible female and I only spent a couple of hours in her company. When was the next time you saw her?"

"I didn't. The next few days were spent rehearsing the *castello* and I was hardly at home. She didn't come back. I can be sure of that because we practise on the football field and I can see my house."

He lapsed into silence and poured more lemonade.

"This is very good," said Mia.

He looked into his glass as if seeing it for the first time. "Yes, it is. My sister is like me. We don't buy the supermarket stuff but make our own. Here and now I feel balanced again. The argument with the Suarez woman affected me badly. I had headaches, my concentration was no longer sharp and I woke early in the mornings with a conviction something bad was going to happen."

"And Saturday? Talk me through your day, step by step." Beatrice watched the man fold his hands as if in prayer.

"I woke up about four with another headache. I drank some iced tea and took a shower. When it got light, I made breakfast: pan tostada, eggs, coffee and orange juice. The weather forecast said sunny and hot, so I wanted to be full of energy. I dressed in my costume, filled my water bottle from the well and walked into town to catch the bus with my colleagues. Núria was one of the first to see me and she came over immediately. She and Joan were in full support over my suspension of their son, Raimon. They told me he was grounded and would not be attending the *festa*. A good woman. A good mother." He crossed himself and kept his eyes on the ground.

Mia and Beatrice waited until he was ready to continue. The cat emerged from under the camellia bush, its black fur dusted with pollen and settled in the middle of the path to wash itself.

"We got out at Plaça de la Vila, practised our music in the back street and joked around to calm our nerves. I remember seeing you there, Mia. Then on the signal, we marched into the square and got into formation. It was exactly as we rehearsed. Note perfect. I was so happy, euphoric that we had come this far. A little light-headed, perhaps, but I put it down to pride in Sirenes and its people. Carlos asked me if I was having a hot flush, I was so red in the face. The sun was powerful and I had forgotten to drink so I emptied my water bottle in three gulps. We set up the base of the *castello*, I climbed up Marco's back and we were solid as a row of bricks. Until ..."

He drank his glass of lemonade.

"I don't know what it was. The pressure on my shoulders, the sweat on my back and the sun in my eyes, I could stand it all, as I do every year. Then my body just quit. I had no muscles, no bones, no strength and my vision narrowed to a pinprick. Next thing I knew, I woke up in hospital."

Mia reached out a hand and touched his elbow. "We're sorry to make you relive all this."

He looked up, his face stricken. "If I fainted, I am ashamed for not recognising the signs. If I passed out because I am too old and unfit, I am sorry I didn't retire earlier. But the one thing I will swear on the soul of my dear departed wife is that I consumed no alcohol, drugs or any other mind-altering substances. I was one hundred percent clean, that much I know. But it doesn't bring Joan's wife back or return Raimon's mother. When is the funeral?"

"Friday. Will you come?"

Bertrand closed his eyes. "How could I face those people after what I've done?" He stood up and collected the glasses. "Thank you for trying to help. It was kind of you to visit and I hope you have a nice journey home. Please don't come here again. Goodbye and mind out for the cat."

He had gone inside before either of them could respond.

The sun was on its downward trajectory as the two women descended the hill. With the disappearance of the light and the abrupt ejection from the Gallego villa, Beatrice sensed a cloud of gloom descending.

Mia's face reflected the same, but she knew the man better than Beatrice.

"Do you think he might change his mind? If so, we could stay overnight and try again."

Mia exhaled through her nose. "Bertrand Gallego is as stubborn as a donkey. Let's find your friends and go home. This whole trip was a very scenic waste of time."

10

A peculiar sound, one unfamiliar since she'd been in Spain, woke Beatrice sometime before six in the morning. Rain. Like fingertips tapping on a table top, drops hit the roof, dripped down the drainpipe and swelled the gutters in the street below. She got out of bed to observe the phenomenon, streetlights reflecting off the curtain of precipitation like tinsel.

Getting into bed after watching inclement weather was ten times cosier and she snuggled up with every expectation of falling into a comfortable doze. Then a vision crossed her mind. Water filling all the creeks, rivers, streams and wells.

Phrases battered her brain as if they'd been waiting in the wings.

I threatened to throw her down the well.

She deliberately pollutes the water supply so surveyors undervalue the selling price.

Filled my water bottle from the well

One hundred percent clean, that much I know.

Forgotten to drink so I emptied my water bottle in three gulps.

"Shit!"

She scrambled out of bed, dragged on her dressing gown and rapped on the room next door.

"Will? Are you awake?"

He opened the door in a matter of seconds, blinking and wearing nothing more than his underwear. "What is it?" he whispered.

"I've had a thought. Can I make you a coffee and pick your brains? You might want to put some clothes on. It's a bit too parky for boxer shorts."

Will rubbed his face. "Give me a second."

When he emerged in his tracksuit, she had prepared the coffee and was sitting at the kitchen table, making notes.

"Sorry to drag you out of bed so early."

"That's OK. Once we're done here, I'll go for a run. You said you had a thought?" He reached a banana from the fruit bowl and began peeling.

Beatrice explained her theory and by the time she had finished, Will's eyebrows were practically in his hairline.

"That's pretty outlandish, even for you. Once again, I'm hearing no hard facts, only hearsay. Based on what one resentful man told you, you suspect a professional lawyer of tipping bottles of Smirnoff down his well so that he'd collapse and cause the death of one of his neighbours. I'm not buying it. Looking at it from the supposed perp's perspective, there's way too much that could go wrong! How much would she have to pour down there to make sure he was drunk on the day of the festival? How could she be sure he'd drink it and not taste the alcohol? How did she arrange for him to consume it just before he went up the human tower? I'm not buying it, Beatrice. This time, you're way off base."

"She has form with this kind of thing! She has previously poisoned other water supplies in order to acquire their land."

"That's a matter of police record, is it? Not what some bitter old geezer told you."

Beatrice scowled at him.

"You wanted a sounding-board," he said. "Not my fault if you don't like what you're hearing. Look at this another way. From what you and Mia told us on the way home, I could concoct an equally coherent and possibly less fanciful explanation. This Bertrand bloke has made a name for himself as a non-drinker. Maybe he sticks to that in public. In private, he enjoys the odd tipple until it becomes a habit. He wouldn't be the first authority figure to preach abstinence while doing quite the opposite in his personal life. His drinking is under control until one day it isn't. Sadly, the day it catches up with him is the worst imaginable timing. In disgrace, he runs away from the village and hints at some nefarious plot to poison him."

"When you put it like that, it sounds plausible. But you didn't meet him, Will. He was sincere, I'd swear to that. Haunted eyes and worry lines, the poor man looked wretched."

"So would I if I'd just given up heavy drinking. Add to that a woman's death on your conscience and you'd be none too frisky either. My bet is this: instead of testing that well for traces of alcohol, which you're unlikely to find after almost a week and this downpour, you'd be better off searching his house for empty bottles. But the fact is, you can do neither because you don't have the authority. Or the time, come to that. Tomorrow is our last full day here. Do you really want to spend it ferreting around for non-existent evidence to clear a guy who doesn't even want to be absolved?"

Beatrice said nothing. His logic was irrefutable.

His tone softened. "If you genuinely think there's something to investigate, take your theory to the police. Who knows, maybe the lawyer woman already has a record and this will give them a reason to arrest her and raid her offices?" He stood up and stretched. "I'm going for a run along the beach. Promise me one thing?"

"No going down wells?"

"Ding dong." He gave her the thumbs-up. "See you in an hour. Eggs and bacon would be lovely, thanks very much."

Adrian, to Beatrice's chagrin, agreed with his husband.

"Don't get me wrong, I can totally believe Ona Suarez is capable of tampering with someone's water supply to get rid of them. Cold-blooded cow. That said, the last thing PI Stubbs should be doing is poking around deserted houses and falling down wells. If I'd known there was such a thing on the property, I'd never have left you alone. Who has wells these days? I mean, it's like the plot of an Agatha Christie novel. The point is, we have a day and a half left in Spain and just over a week before we land in Paris. We should focus our minds on how to enjoy today and what to wear next Sunday."

"Cows are warm-blooded. I have no intention of poking around any holes in the ground, I can assure you. All I want to do before we leave is deliver my findings to the authorities. Failing that, I'll hand it over to Mia."

Will, freshly showered and glowing with health, made a noise of disagreement, but couldn't speak until he'd swallowed his forkful of egg on toast. "Who are the police more likely to believe? An ex-detective with her own agency or an ex-model with a clothing line? Call Mia, get an appointment with a detective and tell him or her everything you know. We'll come with you on the train and after you're done, we can have lunch in Vilanova i la Geltrú. I'd like to see the place."

"Me too!" Adrian beamed.

"And those of us who are up to it can walk back."

Adrian wrinkled his nose.

"Up to you, of course" Will cut more bread. "But the coastal path goes past the nudist beaches."

Adrian hesitated. "Well, let's see how we feel. Should I look up some restaurant tips?"

"Wait a minute," Beatrice interjected. "Mia is an ex-model with a clothing line? How the hell do you know that and I don't?"

"I asked. Last night, while you and Adrian were flat out in the back seat, she and I had a nice chat about her former career, life in Salisbury and the challenges of setting up a clothing business in today's climate. She's an impressive woman. I can see why you two get on."

"Makes sense," said Adrian. "She has stunning bone structure. I wonder if she does menswear?"

"I'll ask," said Beatrice, folding her napkin and reaching for her phone.

To her surprise, Mia was underwhelmed by the idea of going to the police, but agreed to make the appointment. Her downbeat tone encouraged Beatrice to take the call outside so they could speak in confidence.

"If you'd rather not come with me, I completely understand. Yesterday took the wind out of my tails, so I know how you feel. It's as if Bertrand is giving up."

"He already has. The mayor called me this morning. He received formal notification that Bertrand Gallego has agreed to sell his home and land, including the football field to Suarez y Chan. He will sign the contracts next week. We're too late, Beatrice. She defeated him and got what she wanted. Anyway, I'll fix a time to see the police and thank you for the lunch invitation. One last meal with you and your friends would be a pleasure. I'm sad to see you go."

A wild impulse seized Beatrice and she spoke without thinking. "If I were to stay on a few days, just to see this through, would you happen to know of a decent hotel?"

The police inspector was a no-nonsense woman whose frown lifted when Mia explained Beatrice's background. Arms folded on the table, she listened to Beatrice's précis of the situation and Mia's translation with equal attention. Her junior was less discreet, her side-eyes and raised brows evidence of her cynicism as she noted key elements of their testimony.

Inspector Vinolas heard them out, blinked twice and without checking her colleague's notes, had questions of her own.

"If Señor Gallego feels a victim of a crime, why does he not report it?"

"What do you expect me and my colleagues to do about your accusation?"

"What evidence do you have that someone added alcohol to his drinking supply?"

"Are there cameras recording activity outside his house or on his football field?"

"Did Señora Stubbs conduct her interview with Señora Suarez with full transparency? No deception involved?"

"Do you have any examples of how Suarez y Chan acquired land through unethical or illegal means?"

Each question chastened them both until they were reduced to shaking their heads. The inspector gave them an even stare and spoke in a calm, sympathetic voice. Beatrice could only take in the tone and body language until Mia delivered the translation.

"She thanks us for our time. The officers have taken note of our interest but without proof or a statement from the complainant, she can see no way forward. Blocking the sale of Bertrand's land or testing the quality of his water is outside her remit and in any case, she has no justification. If we discover anything more to substantiate our claims, she is willing to listen. Her final comment is that she appreciates and admires our determination."

The inspector backed up Mia's words with a kind smile, but that didn't stop Beatrice from feeling like a dotty old bat who reported a pumpkin spoiler to the judge of a village show. The junior officer showed them out, no doubt to burst into hysterical laughter the moment the door was closed.

"I feel foolish and I made you look foolish too. I'm sorry." Beatrice hung her head.

Mia took her arm and they crossed the road together. "Something tells me that is not true. Vinolas has a reputation for being brusque and impatient. Today, she was attentive and kind. I have a feeling our words will resonate and trigger some understated activity. We are unlikely to see it, but certain ears pricked up at what we said. You didn't hear her words thanks to my hurried translation. She asked us 'What do you expect me to do?' Then she detailed everything a good officer would do if pursuing this case. I feel anything but foolish. We did the right thing. Take heart, my friend, and let's enjoy our lunch by the sea."

"Do you think so? Really?"

"Really. If she thought us foolish, we'd have been out of there in five minutes. We had an interview lasting over half an hour. I say again, we did the right thing. Turn right here, the hotel is on the next corner. My friend Elias runs this place. He has a room you can rent at a discount, if you want to stay."

Beatrice thought it over as they strolled below palm trees and gazed out at the sea. "It's Núria's funeral tomorrow, right? I might stay on another day or two, if your friend can spare me a room. My gut tells me this isn't over. The thing is, if Bertrand has sold his property, she's won."

"If is a very big word. We have time to block this sale and save Sirenes. With or without Bertrand's help. Oh, look, there's the best-looking couple in Sitges!"

Adrian was waving from a blue and white terrace, gesturing at the beach, the umbrellas and the location of their table in prime position.

"Someone's used her influence!" he gushed, kissing Mia on both cheeks. "This place is divine and Vilanova as a whole is a treasure. We just came from the Pasifaë sculpture. OMG! Now I'm all impassioned about Greek myths." He kissed Beatrice, ushered them into padded seats and poured them a glass of fizz. "We ordered a Corpinnat, what else? How did it go at the cop shop?"

"The jury's out," said Beatrice. "But I've decided to stay a few more days. I promise not to fall in any wells or antagonise cold-blooded cows, but I can't leave here without having another stab at the truth. Mia's going to arrange me a room at this hotel and I'll rebook my flight. Do you mind?"

She looked at Will's sunglasses. His eyes were shaded but his expression was warm.

"We don't mind. Mia, I know this is an impossible request, but would you please try to keep Beatrice Stubbs out of trouble? Cheers!"

11

What with one thing and another, Friday was a highly emotional day. Will, Adrian and Beatrice packed up their things and cleaned their little apartment, all of them sorry to leave. They had breakfast in La Paloma café opposite the station. Will said very little, stirring his coffee morosely. Adrian battered Beatrice with a stream of questions, as if she was wholly incompetent at managing her own affairs.

"You changed your flight to Monday, right? So who's looking after Huggy Bear?"

"She's staying where she is. Gabriel and Tanya are always happy to have a dog in the house. Yes, my flight is rearranged for Monday, but I paid a bit extra in case I want to extend till the end of the week."

"The end of the week?" Adrian's voice went to a high C. "Beatrice, Catinca's show is next Saturday in Paris and you cannot just turn up in a linen dress and a pair of flip-flops. Stop me if I've mentioned this before, but we will be in the front row. Front. Row. Paris." He mimed blowing air kisses and filming the catwalk. "Gwyneth, I love that colour on you, babe! Hi, Timothée, rocking the vintage boots!" He plucked at his shirt and rolled his eyes. "What, this old thing?"

"Don't call me an old thing." Beatrice caught Will's eye and got the first grin of the day.

Adrian narrowed his eyes. "That was faux-modesty to describe my edgy yet effortless attire. The point is ..."

"I see. So you've got an outfit in mind for yourself?"

"For myself *and* my husband. We're going to slay the paparazzi. That's another thing. Who's going to be your plus one? I bet Marianne would love it but you'd better let her know ASAP."

Beatrice smiled. Her god-daughter would indeed love the glitz and glamour of a Parisian fashion show. But Beatrice had someone else in mind. "Are you applying for the job of my personal assistant? If so, you've failed the interview because I'm looking for someone less bossy. I think I'll have another coffee. They're awfully good."

"I agree," said Adrian. "I'll join you."

"If you really want another and not just an excuse to bully Beatrice, get one to go. The train leaves in fifteen minutes and we have to get tickets yet. Don't give me that look. You're the one who wanted to get the early train so we have plenty of time in Duty Free."

They abandoned the idea of coffee and Beatrice dragged her case across the road to see them off. Adrian always got tearful over goodbyes, even though she'd be seeing him in a week, so she wasn't surprised to see him dabbing his eyes. When Will choked up, it was more of a shock.

He hugged her tightly and murmured into her hair. "I promised Matthew I'd look after you, not abandon you in a foreign country on a wild goose chase. I have a bad feeling about this." He released her but gripped her shoulders and looked her in the eye. "Take no risks, OK?"

She swallowed her own emotions. "I swear. Safe trip and see you Monday."

They passed through the ticket barriers and with a last wave, walked off to find their platform. Beatrice checked the screens. The next train to Vilanova was in twenty-five minutes. Plenty of time for another coffee.

Whether it was the extra shot of caffeine or the clarity permitted by solitude, Beatrice acknowledged the fact she had missed something. Yesterday, in the interview with the police inspector, no one had mentioned the hospital report on Bertrand Gallego. Surely medical tests would indicate what kind of intoxication the man had been under. It was incredibly frustrating to ask questions, wait for the translation, listen to the answer in Catalan and only then hear it in English. No wonder her analytical thinking was slower than usual.

The inspector was a pro and would be unlikely to share any information with her or Mia. However, the question might nudge the woman to pursue that line of enquiry. Beatrice could have kicked herself. The chances of the police giving them another half hour was negligible. The first thing the desk sergeant would ask was if there was any new proof. There wasn't.

Still furious with herself, she bought her ticket to Vilanova i la Geltrú and muttered another curse when she saw she had to carry her sizeable case down a set of steps and up the other side to access the correct platform. A voice addressed her in American English.

"Do you need a hand with that?"

She turned to see a tall black man smiling down at her dressed in the most eye-popping outfit. His suit was tangerine-orange, his shirt and tie a shimmery green patterned with snake scales, and his tan shoes were pointy at the toe. He wore his sunglasses on his head.

"If it's no trouble, that would be extremely kind."

"My pleasure." He lifted her bag, whose weight had caused Iron Man to grunt as he hefted it down the stairs that morning, with as much ease and delicacy as if it were a basket of eggs. "Platform 3? I guess you're heading to Tarragona."

"Vilanova i la Geltrú, actually. It's only one stop. Do you know it at all?"

"No, I can't say I do. Would you recommend the place?" He kept pace with her, her suitcase in his right hand and his left arm bent at the elbow in case she needed extra support. If she had been seeking a personal assistant, he would fit the bill perfectly.

"Oh, yes, wholeheartedly. One can even walk there along the beach path, I hear. Not that I've tried. I hope you don't mind my saying but your clothes are quite wonderful. Seeing you would gladden the heart of the most wretched soul."

His laugh reverberated around the tunnel. "I appreciate the compliment. When I woke up this morning, I said to myself, Clarence, today is the day to dress like a Seville Orange." He laughed again and Beatrice joined in. "In return, may I say your accent is music to my ears. Sit me down with an English costume drama and I won't bother nobody. Downton Abbey, Bridgerton, anything by Jane Austen, I can't get enough."

They climbed up the steps and emerged into the sunshine of Platform 3. Few people were waiting for the train but those who were could not take their eyes from Clarence. He wheeled the suitcase along to an empty bench and gestured for Beatrice to take a seat.

"You're extremely kind and I am most grateful. A gentleman like yourself would fit right into a period piece where manners maketh the man. Before you sit down, might I be so bold to ask another favour? A friend of mine is in a terrific flap about what to wear to a fashion show next weekend. In my eyes, you're an absolute inspiration. Will you permit me to take a photograph? I shan't share it with anyone else, you have my word."

"It would be an honour." He struck a pose like a pro, one hand in his pocket, right knee bent and the other arm relaxed by his side.

Beatrice took several shots, offering advice so she could get every angle. "That's utterly wonderful, thank you, Clarence. By the way, my name is Beatrice."

He sat beside her, hitching up his trousers at the knee. "Well, I am very pleased to make your acquaintance, Beatrice. Tell me more about this fashion show. Is it in Barcelona on Sunday evening? Because I might be at the same event, wearing a box-fresh suit."

"Ooh, you're a fashionista too! Or maybe that's the wrong term for a man. No, this one is in Paris next Saturday morning. We've got front row seats and Adrian – that's my flapping friend – thinks we have to outdo all the models. To tell you the truth, Clarence, I wish I could just watch from backstage and avoid all the pomp."

He took his sunglasses off his head and stuck one of the arms in his mouth, his expression thoughtful. "On the front row, people will see three things and in this order: your outfit, your jewellery and your shoes. Plus make-up, sunglasses, handbags, etcetera." He gave her an appraising once-over. "Wear some-thing classic and comfortable in navy blue, accessorise with your best bling and get a pair of wedge boots. Carry a piece by the designer, such as a jacket or shawl, to show good manners, but be yourself."

A tannoy announcement informed them the next departure to Tarragona was imminent.

"Excellent advice. I feel far less panicky now. What will you be wearing to your do in Barcelona?" She had to raise her voice over the sound of the incoming train.

"That's the best kept secret in fashion! Let me take your bag."

He escorted her onto the train, tucked her suitcase beside her seat and saluted. "Have a great time at the show, Beatrice. Look fabulous for me!"

"You're not travelling on this train?"

"Nope. I'm off to Barcelona for a fitting. Just wanted to be sure you got your ride. *Hasta luego.*" With that, he saluted and dashed out of the doors as the whistle blew.

For a few minutes, Beatrice puzzled over a random man's patience and generosity, even checking her phone to make sure the shots she'd taken were real. Then she sat back and smiled. Angels didn't always wear white. Sometimes they wore Seville Orange.

Dear Adrian, inspiration struck when I met this extraordinary young man this morning. Isn't he a head-turner? I think you should wear something like this. You can barely see his shoes in any of these shots but they were very pointy. Bx

Beaches and sea flashed by and before she could write another text message to Will exhorting him not to worry, the train pulled in to Vilanova i la Geltrú. She heaved her suitcase out of the carriage and was already exhausted by the time she'd wheeled it down the long platform to the station itself. Outside, she spotted a taxi and asked the driver to take her to Hotel Nero.

During the ten-minute drive to the hotel, her phone pinged with three increasingly puzzling text messages from Adrian.

"Hahaha! You think I could get away with a du Ciel suit?!?!"

"That looks like Sitges station. When did you learn to Photoshop?"

"Don't tell me you actually met CdC! I am going to throw myself onto the tracks the minute I get the window open. Beatrice! ANSWER ME!"

She had no idea how to respond and her battery was low, so she sat back to enjoy the beachside on the way to the hotel. Ocean views lifted the spirits, everyone knew that. Her spirits would need a great deal of lifting before she attended this afternoon's funeral.

Her room was a corner suite, with a V-shaped French window overlooking the beach. Mia must have called in a lot of favours to get such a wonderful room at short notice. She unpacked her grey suit, left the suitcase open and plugged her phone in to charge.

Immediately, she had five notifications. All missed calls from Adrian.

She pressed his number.

"Beatrice Stubbs, are you deliberately trying to infuriate me? If so, it's working."

"Not the slightest. I met a chap at the station, admired his outfit and asked if I could take a picture. He was quite charming, even to the point of carrying my case onto the train. He said his name was Clarence, that's all I can tell you. Oh, another thing is that he has a fashion show in Barcelona on Sunday."

Adrian was hyperventilating or some such dramatics at the other end of the line.

"Adrian, speak to me. Are you trying to say he's someone famous I should know? Because he gave no air of 'Do you know who I am?' and celebrities don't usually offer to carry my case."

"I do *not* believe this. On the first day we arrived in Sitges, I overheard another couple gossiping. Clarence du Ciel was in town. Several sightings, apparently. From that moment, I was on high alert but didn't catch a glimpse of the man. Less than an hour after I packed up and shipped out, you not only meet him but you made him carry your suitcase. Are you doing your faux naiveté thing or did you genuinely not recognise him?"

"How on earth am I supposed to recognise someone I've never heard of? Where are you? It's very noisy."

"Checking in. Tell me you got his card, at the very least."

"It never occurred to me. Now listen, I need to get dressed and go to this funeral. Have fun in Duty Free and talk to you soon. Bye bye."

Adrian merely groaned so Beatrice rang off. He was such a drama queen.

12

Once again, the grey suit. It had seen her through so much: police briefings, funerals, witness interviews, client meetings and even a polo match. Wherever she travelled, it came too. Today it was at its sober best, paired with a white blouse and plain black court shoes. With a little mascara on her eyelashes and a slick of lip salve, she was ready to go. Although she'd never met the woman who died, she tucked a packet of tissues into her handbag. These days, she cried very easily.

Mia was already in Sirenes, so Beatrice took the bus alone. Today, Carlotta was driving. She gave Beatrice a cursory nod and asked for no fare. With a grateful smile; Beatrice sat on the side of the bus which faced the ocean and steeled herself for the wringer of the afternoon.

They trundled out of Vilanova y la Geltrú, past already familiar sights, such as the endlessly swimming mermaids. Today, she noted both the sirens were wearing black arm bands. The square, busier than she had ever seen it, was occupied by small groups of black-clad people, talking in low voices. Beatrice got off the bus and stood awkwardly near the fountain, wondering where she was supposed to go. The village itself was peculiarly silent for the number of people present. Amid the sea of black suits and hats, she couldn't locate Mia or any other face she recognised.

While she was waiting in the shadow of the hotel, she saw Carlotta pick up her handbag and prepare to leave the bus. Waiting at the stop was one of her colleagues, a young man with very short hair in the bus company uniform. Carlotta descended the steps but blocked his entrance. She lit a cigarette and then released a lecture in just over a whisper but with ferocious emphasis and gritted teeth. The replacement driver held up his hands in defence but she continued to glower at him from beneath her brows. Eventually he conceded and took a step backwards. Only then did she let him on the bus. The passengers, an attentive audience in a shambolic queue, thanked Carlotta as she walked past and into the hotel bar.

"Beatrice." Mia was walking up the pavement towards her, elegant in a black velvet dress, kitten heels and a well cut brocade jacket. "You came. I wondered if you had changed your mind. Let's walk this way. The whole village will be in the church so you and I should join those outside to listen to the service through a loudspeaker. People have come from all around to pay their respects. It's going to be busy."

The two women took a side street towards the church. Outside the main door, there were a row of benches, already filling up with mourners. Mia found a seat and immediately bowed her head to pray. Out of a desire to display good manners, Beatrice followed suit, although she had no interest in religion.

A rustle of clothes and whispers attracted her attention. Joan Soler and his son Raimon came through the gate, heads bent and eyes on the ground. The priest met them in the doorway and ushered them inside. The general fidgeting and impatience stilled to a respectful silence. Every person in the congregation, inside the building and out in the graveyard, was trying to imagine how it must feel for Joan to lose his wife at such a young age. How must it feel for Raimon, already battling with his teenage troubles, to lose his mother? The sky stayed blue and the sun shone as strongly as ever but a chill blew over the graveyard.

Even though Beatrice understood very little of the ceremony, the key points were obvious. Núria Soler was a decent woman, loved and respected by her family, friends and neighbours. She died doing something which mattered to her every bit as being a good wife and mother. That role was being part of the community. Around Beatrice, people reached for their tissues and bowed their heads to their hands. They stood and prayed, they sat and listened to the music chosen by her family and finally commended her to God.

The church doors opened to reveal the priest followed by six men bearing the coffin. Beatrice's breath caught when she realised both Joan and Raimon were two of the bearers. By now, people were openly weeping. A sad shuffle of people fell into line after the churchgoers and were still taking their place by the time the priest was ready to inter the body. Joan and his son threw roses into the grave and scattered earth on the wood. An older woman Beatrice guessed was Núria's mother tried to do the same but stumbled and fell, caught by two men. Her sobs were agonising.

The ceremony of paying respects to the deceased and the bereaved relatives took nearly forty minutes. It was heartening to see how many young people stepped up to say a few quiet words or simply bow their heads at the graveside. Beatrice scanned the crowd for any sign of Bertrand Gallego but she could identify no one in a sea of black suits. Mia nudged her and indicated it was time to join the line.

"Should I?" whispered Beatrice. "I feel like an interloper and I don't believe Joan Soler will be pleased to see me. You go ahead. I'll wait right here."

"No, come. Joan is one of the people who wants to employ you. Come and do the necessaries. It matters."

They stood in line until they reached the wan-looking father and son. Mia went first, shaking hands and whispering condolences. Beatrice shook Raimon's hand and muttered, "I'm so sorry." His response was a stony look. In contrast, Joan's face took on more animation once he saw Beatrice move into his eye line.

"I'm so very sorry," she said. "I wish there was something I could do."

He clasped her hand in both of his. "I apologise for our last meeting, I was rude. There is something you can do and we are willing to pay for it. Stay for the hospitality, please. We want to talk to you."

He didn't wait for an answer and turned to the person waiting behind her. To Beatrice's surprise, it was Carlotta, dressed in sombre black.

On Mia's advice, they stopped for a drink at the café opposite before attending the wake. As soon as they crossed the road, Beatrice could see they were not the only ones. A crowd of people spilled from the little bar into the street, all wearing black and many shaking their heads or smoking.

"We let the family go first. Everyone else has a drink and offloads their experiences before we join them. It helps soften the blow. This was one of the biggest funerals I've ever seen in Sirenes. It doesn't surprise me. Everyone knew Núria, as a mother, a bakery worker, wife and an organiser. I used to tease her, calling her Núria Non-stop. She ran so many community meetings, I don't know how she kept up. It must be strange for Joan and Raimon to see their grief shared by so many."

"Strange, but comforting. The numbers of people are testament to how well she and her family were loved. I wish I could have met her."

Mia poured the little carafe of red wine into two glasses. "You can do the second best thing. You can see her through our eyes. Beatrice, I warn you, Joan and the two men we interviewed last week have raised enough money to pay a professional investigator. We want you. We know you're retired, we know you feel hobbled by your inability to speak Catalan, but you are invested. You were there. I will say no more but be prepared for an ambush by some of the villagers at the wake. Do you like the wine? It's a Rioja."

The sudden switch from *they*, the villagers to *we*, the villagers put Beatrice on the back foot. She sipped the wine, focusing on the final question in order to let her mind catch up.

"It's excellent. As a matter of fact and with no disrespect to this region, Rioja is one of my favourites. We have history together. Mia, I should say that I am not here in a professional capacity, nor am I looking for employment. You are right to say I'm invested in the outcome but I have zero faith in the process. I can't take this any further because I don't have the authority. You must see that, surely? You were there at the interview with the police yesterday. If they can't prove anything, I don't have a bat's chance in hell. That's why I couldn't possibly take your neighbours' money because I can't deliver what they're paying me to do. If I could, nothing would make me happier. But I can't."

Mia sniffed at her glass. "I too had a love affair with Rioja. Sometimes when I taste a glass, it's like coming face-to-face with an old flame. I do understand your reticence and yet I ask you to listen to what they have to say. It's more than avenging Núria's death. This is about the entire village."

· · ·

If Beatrice had any doubt regarding her anonymity, the moment she walked into the village hall dispelled any such illusion. Everyone turned, stared, and began whispering. Mia guided Beatrice to the central table and introduced half a dozen people with unpronounceable names. Then she did exactly the same at another three tables. Beatrice's face was beginning to hurt from all the smiling. One woman pointed at the buffet table and clapped her hands as if to hurry them up. That suited Beatrice down to the ground. She loaded a paper plate with some oily peppers, a slice of tortilla, a mini fish kebab and a spicy-looking salsa. While Mia was still picking and choosing, Beatrice found an empty table and unbuttoned her suit jacket. Instantly, she was surrounded by half a dozen people.

Joan Soler sat opposite her, flanked by his son, the mayor, the two men they had interviewed the previous week, and Carlotta.

"Sorry to interrupt. Please, eat your meal." Joan's gestures would have communicated this message without the words spoken in English. His colleagues nodded their agreement and wafted their hands towards her plate, as if to transport the delicacies into her mouth.

"I know what you are going to say and I apologise in advance for my refusal. I cannot solve this case alone. The police have more intelligence than I do. If you have any information that sheds light on your wife's death, you must take it to the authorities."

All six of them stared at her, only breaking their gaze when Mia came to join the table. "You started without me? Beatrice, have these people explained exactly what they want you to do and how much they are prepared to pay you for the task?"

Beatrice ate a mouthful of salsa and wish she'd started with the fish kebab. Food impeded speech but encouraged thought. "To be honest, we barely got started. Would you like to fill me in? Please sit down."

The group fetched more chairs and sat at the table, watching Beatrice eat. She noted that it wasn't just the people at the table whose eyes were on her, but everyone in the room was unable to hide their interest.

"Joan? The floor is yours," said Mia.

"Thank you. Will you translate for everyone else?"

"Of course."

"Beatrice, nothing can bring my wife and Raimon's mother back. We know that. Just as we know there was something very wrong about the circumstances of her death. On top of that, losing Bertrand and our football field will destroy this village. We can't let that happen. The mayor and I have collected enough contributions to pay someone to help us and we want that person to be you. You were already investigating, inter- viewing people and travelling north to meet Bertrand. All we ask is that you continue and we will pay for your time."

Raimon glowered at her from under his brows with that mixture of rage and contempt only a teenager can truly muster while Mia translated Joan's words.

"I understand," said Beatrice. "The fact is, my investigation has hit a brick wall. I took what I learned to the police. I can do no more."

Raimon stood up sharply and his chair clattered to the floor. He said something guttural and made a dismissive gesture before stalking out of the room. Everyone fell silent.

"I'm sorry about that," said Joan. "He's taking everything hard. He and his mother had an argument before she left for Vilanova and he blames himself. He's not the only one. I blame myself for *not* being there and everyone who *was* there feels in some way responsible. But the one person no one blames is Bertrand Gallego."

Mia translated and all heads first nodded sadly then shook with emphasis.

"The village needs Bertrand. We are one hundred percent behind him and we want him to stay. If he really feels it's time for him to leave, we would be sad, but we would support his decision. But not like this. Selling his land because he takes responsibility for Núria's death is wrong on every level. You must help us, Beatrice. You must find out what happened."

Dozens of pairs of eyes bored into her and the pressure was immense.

"Look, I agree to stay another week and find out what I can. You understand that may be nothing at all and if that is the case, you don't owe me a penny. Or cent, to be more accurate." Her mind strayed to Bertrand's well. "If there is money available, we might want to spend it on doing a few tests. The reason the police don't take my theories seriously is due to a lack of proof. That's why I am going to need some local assistance."

When Mia had finished relaying her words, there was a round of applause and a clamour of offers to help, with people shoving their way closer to the table to volunteer.

Joan held up a hand for silence. "You can have as much assistance as you want. Where shall we start?"

"We start," said Beatrice, "with the well."

In a matter of minutes, the wake transformed into mission control. To Beatrice's eyes, the scene was total chaos, but gradually some kind of organisation emerged. A group of people removed all the food and set it on the bar. Others arranged tables and chairs in a rough semicircle facing Beatrice, Joan, the mayor et al, as if it was an awards ceremony. A debate ensued as to who should sit at which table until the mayor took charge, his stentorian voice booming orders until everyone was finally settled.

Joan and Mia looked to Beatrice for instructions. She stared into her wine glass for a moment and imagined she was addressing an operations room at Scotland Yard.

"The important thing is to pursue several lines of enquiry." The pause while Joan translated her words into Catalan was extremely useful, enabling her to think of what she wanted to say next.

"Earlier this week, Mia and I travelled to Cadaqués, where we met Bertrand Gallego. He is a broken man, defeated by something he sees as his fault."

It was easy to see which mourners understood English as their reactions came immediately and others after her words were rendered in Catalan.

"From what Bertrand told us, I believe someone introduced alcohol into his drinking water. That is why I need to take a sample from the well. After the rain, I think it's highly unlikely we will find anything at all. But we must try. Two people should take at least six samples and take them to a laboratory for testing. I say two people because everything we do must be subject to the four-eye principle. If not, anything we discover is open to accusations of corruption."

The furore which broke out after that speech took a good few minutes to settle. Beatrice waited patiently as Joan quietened the villagers and heard one speaker after another. He seemed to make a decision and pointed at three people on one table.

"Oliver and Simon will get samples from the well and take them to Teresa. She is a vet and she has the necessary analytical equipment. Carlotta will accompany her, ensuring an authentic testing system. Is that satisfactory?"

Beatrice tapped her lips. "Yes, that sounds like just the job. While they perform that task, I think we need three other prongs of attack. Firstly, someone needs to talk to Bertrand. I know he doesn't want to speak to anybody but until he hears the people of Sirenes' point of view, he will not appreciate how much faith you have in him and his role in the community."

She expected another wave of willing volunteers when the people heard her words. Instead there was a patient silence, all eyes on Joan.

"That task is mine," he said. "Maybe Mia will come with me, as one of his oldest friends?"

Mia nodded her acceptance.

"There are two other things I believe we can do. Both of them involve appealing to someone's better nature. Firstly, Ona Suarez. She is the woman brokering this deal and the one who has the most to gain from acquiring Bertrand's property. I already met the woman once, so that counts me out. Secondly, the man representing El Castor is called Juan Ferrera. If I can get an audience and someone will assist with the Spanish translation, I will do my best to sway his opinion."

"*Hijos da puta*!" Raimon stood in the doorway of the room, red-faced and gasping out an urgent alert, pointing over his shoulder.

At least half the room reacted by leaping to their feet and rushing outside. Joan laid a calming hand on Beatrice's forearm. "A security team have arrived. They are taping off access to Gallego's property before the land has been sold. It is not right."

Beatrice thought fast. "Just his house or the football field as well?"

"Raimon said the house. Bastards! They knew everyone would be at church today so they're laying claim before the ink is dry on the contract. That means we won't have access to the well. Beatrice, I think we're too late."

A fury built in Beatrice as she considered the shameless move of blocking villagers' access while they were mourning their loss. "It's never too late. In my bones, I know Ona Suarez forced Bertrand's capitulation and I will damn well find a way to prove it. And if she had any hand in your wife's death, no matter how remotely, I'm going to take that bitch down."

A hand gripped her shoulder. She looked up to see Raimon's face. "*Oui.*"

"*Oui? Tu parles le français?*"

His voice was hoarse from shouting and probably crying. "I was speaking English, not French. *We* are going to take that bitch down."

13

Her blue-and-white bedroom was a haven after the stresses of the day. She poured herself a gin and tonic and took it onto the balcony to soak in the evening. The sun had already set and palm fronds fractured the street lights, creating hypnotic patterns across the promenade. To her left, she could see beachside cafés and restaurants gearing up for the evening's activity but her exhaustion lay over her shoulders like a lead blanket. She didn't even have the energy to go down to the hotel restaurant. What she needed was unimpeded thinking time.

That and the analytical, procedural mind of William Quinn. He would be able to shape the amorphous mass of her thoughts into something resembling coherence. Will dealt in facts, distrusting gossip and dismissing passions. Which was a very good attitude for a Metropolitan police detective. But Beatrice was no longer in the service of the Met. She was on her own, trusting her own instincts (fallible), her professional training (outdated), and verbal accounts of every aspect of the case she was investigating (unverified).

Warm wind tousled her hair and her body began to relax. It was a beautiful evening with moonlight reflecting on the sea. No, she decided, she would not call Will. Nevertheless, certain practical arrangements required attention. A promise to stay another week meant rebooking her flight once again, confirming her hotel room until Saturday and updating her family members on her plans. She collected her mobile and the room service menu before returning to the balcony.

Tanya answered on the first ring. "Beatrice! I thought it might be you. How's it going in Spain? When are you coming home?"

Beatrice cleared her throat. "Yes, about that. I have committed myself to staying another week. It's incredibly irresponsible and will probably turn out to be fruitless, but a duty is a duty. My concern is my promise to you. I said I would be away two weeks and on that premise, you agreed to take care of my dog and my house. Now I've extended twice and I'm sure I'm trying your patience."

"Don't be daft," Tanya laughed. "What difference does it make? We'll miss you, of course, but we love having Huggy Bear. If I really wanted to make you jealous, I'd take a photograph of her right now snoring in front of the hearth. Honestly, it's fine if you want to stay another week. Gabriel went over to your cottage yesterday to check the garden, water the plants, and pick up the post. Are you having a good time?"

That question wasn't easy to answer. "Up to a point. I'm so grateful to you and your wonderful husband. Now I have a sudden attack of missing you desperately and needing to be home. Distract me quickly and tell me about Luke and Bailey Mae."

Tanya didn't answer for a moment and Beatrice's pulse began to race.

"Tanya? Is everything all right?"

"Just a sec."

After another silence and some indefinable fumbling, Gabriel spoke. "Hi, Beatrice. Sorry, the little one has just woken up and is screeching her head off for a feed. Give me ten minutes and I'll be doing the same. What's the story? Tanya says you're staying another week."

His voice, as always, soothed Beatrice like a cool hand on her brow. "Yes, that's what I'd like to do if that's all right? I know it's a huge imposition."

"Not at all. Huggy Bear comes with me on my rounds. She loves it. The kids love her. If there's one thing that's persuaded me to get a dog of our own, it's a couple of weeks with that Border terrier. She gets under everyone's defences. One of my chainsaw operators has taken to calling her Marilyn Monroe." His quiet, warm laugh triggered a huge wave of homesickness.

"And the kids?" Beatrice squeaked, closing her eyes to forestall tears.

Gabriel needed no encouragement to enthuse about his children and his wife. Luke was loving school, Bailey Mae was thriving and Tanya was working from home.

"She's taken on most of the domestic stuff over the last month. I'm not sure if I mentioned it before you left but we're battling for control of the forest north of Upton St Nicholas. You remember the lookout point where we found Will that Christmas? It's at the north-east point of a section of woodland. There's a good reason we designated it as a lookout point and that's because the place is teeming with wildlife. A construction company wanted to buy it and create an estate of family homes."

"Yes! I remember you telling me. Did you manage to stop them?"

She could hear the smile in his voice. "We did. Every local business came together to block the purchase. I've spent more time talking to people in the last two weeks than I do in an average year. The verdict came in on Tuesday. The judge agreed that housing development on that section of land would have a negative effect on wildlife, local businesses, tourism and the region's image as a whole. I won't lie, I had a hangover the size of Dartmoor on Wednesday morning."

Beatrice's laughter bubbled up from her stomach. "I'm so proud of you! Congratulations! As soon as I get back, I'm going to buy you and Tanya a bottle of champagne."

"Fair enough. I might feel like drinking alcohol again by then. Don't worry about us at all. The kids are doing fine, Tanya is happy and you know we'll take good care of Huggy Bear. Luke asks about you every day. You should send me a selfie I can show him. You're not getting into any trouble, are you?"

"No, I am trying to be good. Give my love to Luke, Tanya and Bailey Mae. Cuddle Huggy Bear for me and I will see you next weekend. Goodnight, Gabriel and thank you."

She sat for a few minutes, listening to the waves, occasional cars and faint hints of piano music coming from the restaurant below. A small snack and a half bottle of wine would be the perfect antidote to a stressful day, especially if she dined alone in her room. Like Gabriel, she preferred her own company unless it was for a good cause.

A good cause.

This cause couldn't be much better.

She ordered a seafood platter, a bottle of white and started making plans.

Saturday morning filled Beatrice with a sense of potential. Clear blue skies, glorious sunshine, a brisk wind buffeting beachgoers and best of all, breakfast delivered to her room. She craved a decent cup of coffee along with the privacy to put her plans into action. As soon as the church bells chimed eight o'clock, she intended to call Mia to topple the first domino. But at 07.50, just as she was polishing off bacon and scrambled eggs, her phone rang.

"Hello? This is Beatrice Stubbs."

"Mrs Stubbs, here is Raimon Soler. I have two interesting news for you."

"Good morning, Raimon, and thank you for calling. Interesting news? Please, go ahead."

"You wanted that we get samples from the well, yes?"

"Umm, yes, but I understood a security firm were patrolling the property and access to the public was not permitted. I wouldn't want you to break the law."

"I don't break the law, they do. Those shitters don't have no right to block access, not yet. My friends and I made a plan. They do a distraction, I take water from the well. Six samples and four eyes, you said."

Beatrice's mind ran in circles. "That's correct, but..."

"I have took six clean bottles with no contamination because they are, I don't know the word in English, clean for babies."

"Oh yes, sterilised. You filled six sterilised bottles with water from Bertrand Gallego's well?"

"Exactly. Is professional job. I have took them to Teresa, the animal doctor and she is testing in this moment. More interesting is, I find glass, broken glass."

"Hold on a second, Raimon, did you take the samples on your own or was someone else with you?"

Raimon's tone was indignant. "You say four eyes, we do four eyes. I am gone to the well with Father Francis. Everybody trusts a priest, no?"

Beatrice placed a hand over her eyes. "Let me get this straight. Your friends created some kind of distraction to enable you and the priest to enter Bertrand Gallego's property and take water from the well. What kind of distraction, may I ask?"

He laughed. "You don't want to know."

"Good God, this will never hold up in court. What were you saying about glass?"

"Mrs Stubbs, I'm sorry, my English is not good like my father. For getting water from the well, we use *una galleda, un balde*. Is like a big cup, made of plastic. You know?"

"I think so. You mean a bucket? In that shed where the well is, there's a bucket, a black bucket with a chain. I saw it myself."

"Bucket, yes. I put the bucket down the well three times. Every time, I fill two bottles of water. Second time I bring up the bucket, there was glass. I have a light on my hat from my bicycle. I see water, sand and a heavy piece of broken glass. Like the bottom of a bottle. I take it out, very careful, and is now in pocket of Father Francis."

A brief vignette of trying to convey this scientific retrieval of evidence to the police inspector crossed Beatrice's mind and she closed her eyes.

"Raimon, that is extraordinary. I commend your courage and your ingenuity thank you for informing me. Can I ask you not to do anything else until I've spoken to your father? I assume he knows what you've done?"

"No. When I am home, I tell him. Then I go to bed. Have a good day, Mrs Stubbs."

She wished him the same, drank a lukewarm coffee and wondered where on the scale of good to bad news this should be placed. The clock on her phone said 08.05, so she dialled Mia, who was engaged. She was just getting out of the shower when someone knocked on the door.

Through the spyhole, she saw Mia and Joan Soler.

"Good morning," she said, opening the door wide. "I called you around fifteen minutes ago. You are both early worms."

Only then did she notice the shadows under Joan Soler's eyes were darker than ever. "Is everything all right?"

"Beatrice, we're sorry to call on you at such an uncivilised hour. We planned to drive to Cadaqués this morning. The problem is that Raimon has gone missing. He didn't come home at all last night, his mobile goes straight to answerphone and Joan is worried he might have done something stupid."

"Ah, I see. Please, come in. There's no need to worry. Joan, I heard from Raimon about twenty minutes ago, so I assume his phone is switched on again. Why don't you go onto the balcony and give him a call? Mia and I will organise some coffee."

Joan didn't move. "He called you this morning? What for?"

"To tell me what he had achieved last night. I really would prefer it if he told you himself. Rest assured, he's absolutely fine. Whether what he did could be described as stupid or not, I will leave that up to you. The one thing I will say is your son is one exceptionally brave young man."

Joan looked as if he was about to cry but he stepped through the French windows onto the balcony and closed the doors. Mia and Beatrice watched him take out his phone.

"Raimon is fine, really. Have a seat and a coffee, there should be some left in the pot. Does Bertrand know you're going to visit?"

Mia shook her head. "No, but his sister does. I've known her since I was engaged to her brother."

Beatrice stopped in the act of towelling her hair. "You and Bertrand were engaged?"

"It was a long time ago." Mia looked out of the window where Joan was pacing the balcony, his phone pressed to her ear. "We were too young and too stupid, like so many couples rushing to grow up. Then I met the man who would be my husband and I broke it off. At the time, Bertrand took it very badly. In fact, we only started speaking again after I returned from Salisbury. His sister, however, is more pragmatic. We used to write to each other about once a month with general news and gossip. Until life got in the way and we lost touch. Celia has always been a night owl so I took a chance and called her late last night. She understands why we need to speak to Bertrand. She gave me her assurance he will be there when we arrive. Joan and I were prepared to leave Sirenes at seven o'clock. But Raimon stayed out all night and Joan, the poor man, has had no sleep at all."

"In that case, it's pure insanity to drive a five-hour round trip!"

"I know. When I heard what had happened, I called Jesus."

Beatrice blinked twice. "Jesus?"

"He's a taxi driver for hire. We left him downstairs, having a cigarette. If everything is all right with Raimon, Jesus will drive us to Cadaqués."

Beatrice flapped a hand at the leftovers of her breakfast and went to get dressed. It seemed that every corner she turned, more secrets were waiting in the shadows. She dragged a brush through her hair and reconsidered her plan. It could still work so long as they managed to speak to Bertrand. After learning that Mia was an old flame, Beatrice could think of no one better than her and Joan Soler as the most persuasive partnership.

When she came out of the bathroom, Joan was standing by the window, sipping orange juice. "My boy. Bull-headed, disobedient, brilliant and determined. From what he tells me, Beatrice, he did what you asked. To talk the priest into breaking and entering, my God!" He rubbed his eyes. "Depending on what Teresa finds in the water, we might have some proof."

Beatrice could not suppress a giggle. "The priest was a masterstroke. He really took my chain of evidence comment seriously. Did he mention the broken glass?"

"Yes. I was just telling Mia. I can't believe Father Francis carried it home in his cassock! Well, now I know my boy is safe at home, I'm ready to drive to Cadaqués and beg Bertrand Gallego not to sell his land."

"Good. I have absolute faith in the pair of you. There's just one little change to the plan. Use all your powers of persuasion to do the opposite. You must convince Bertrand to sell."

14

Since the first day she'd first come to Vilanova i la Geltrú, Beatrice had intended to visit the Pasifaë sculpture. That was yet to happen as something always got in the way. When she woke early to clear skies and an empty beach, she seized the chance to pay homage to the beast, the myth and the moment.

Her sunglasses proved their worth by deflecting grains of whirling sand from her eyes and the new cashmere wrap kept her cosy against the sea air. She passed the half-built beach bars, her focus on the iconic image against the sea. To be here alone was a privilege and worth getting out of bed just after the sun had risen.

From a distance, the artwork reminded her of the mermaids of Sirenes. The oxidised metal, graceful arches and the dynamic silhouette against the ocean had striking similarities. But the closer Beatrice drew to the plinth bearing Pasifaë, the more differences she discerned. This mythical creature contained a story in itself. With the horns of a bull and the udder of a cow, its inside was hollow, revealing the writhing form of a woman in ecstasy.

"Pasifaë," whispered Beatrice, although there was no one to hear her words. She recalled the first time she heard the story, sitting on an autumnal bench outside the British Museum, curled against Matthew's tweedy shoulder.

"Pasifaë, daughter of Helios the sun god, was a prized beauty and a goddess of witchcraft. Bear in mind, Old Thing, the Greek Gods tended to the patriarchal, not to mention vengeful. Only a son of Zeus deserved such a treasure and thus Pasifaë was given to Minos, who became King of Crete. Things went a bit sour after a fracas with Poseidon, god of the sea. Historians are still debating the details but Poseidon demanded the sacrifice of an extraordinary white bull. Who knows why, the Greek Gods were a rum lot. Anyway, Minos refused. Poseidon's revenge was to make Pasifaë fall in love with the bull. One can see whence Shakespeare purloined his ideas.

"Poor Pasifaë, driven wild with desire for the animal, persuaded Daedalus to create a fake cow in which she would conceal herself and mate with the beast. You remember Daedalus? He and his son Icarus, who flew too close to the sun? Same chap. The bull was fooled and did indeed mate with the lovely Pasifaë, and the result of their union was the Minotaur. Half man, half bull, he fed on human flesh."

Beatrice walked three times around the sculpture and whilst admiring its power and elegance, she had to agree with Matthew. The Greek Gods were indeed a rum lot.

The next stage of the Sirenes operation was hampered by the language issue. Beatrice waited for the bus as usual, her brand new dictionary in her handbag. It would be enough to start with, but she had no hope of pressing home her message without the help of either a fluent Catalan or Castilian Spanish speaker. Mia or Joan would have been ideal, but they were otherwise engaged in Cadaqués.

The bus pulled in with Carlotta at the wheel. She saluted Beatrice and even cracked a smile as she got out for her customary cigarette. She offered the packet to Beatrice.

"*No, gracias, non fumo.*"

Carlotta's eyes narrowed. "*Tú hablas español.*"

"*No, non hablo español y necesito un traductor.*" She hoped her pronunciation was accurate and she wasn't inadvertently requesting a tractor.

"*Vale.* Don't worry. Get on."

For the first time on this journey, Beatrice paid no attention to the view. She mentally rehearsed her speech in English and made notes using her dictionary towards a translation. Her frustration built as she knew how more persuasive and eloquent either Mia or Joan would be, but she was on her own. Even if the two of them arrived back from Cadaqués by mid-afternoon it would already be too late. Somehow, Beatrice had to galvanise the citizens of Sirenes into action this morning.

Her pulse fluttered because she realised how much there was to do and how under-confident she was of achieving it. She looked up and out of the window just in time to see the mermaid sculpture, the sirens themselves. Those graceful, scaly bodies somehow transferred a pulse of energy through the windows of the bus and Beatrice clenched her fists. She could do this. *Pull yourself together and woman up.*

On arrival in the main square, Carlotta beckoned Beatrice to follow into the same hotel where she and Mia had conducted their first interviews. Inside, the mayor was waiting at a table near the back, flanked by two teenagers, evidently siblings, judging by their strawberry-blonde colouring.

"Beatrice Stubbs," said Carlotta, as if she was delivering a package and stomped off to the bar.

"Good morning," said Beatrice, as all three people stood to greet her. She shook the mayor's hand and said "*Buenos dias, muchas gracias*", then promptly ran out of steam.

The girl stretched out a hand with a confident smile. "Good morning, Mrs Stubbs. My name is Zuzu and this is my twin brother, Pedro. We're both university students and we have volunteered to translate for you today."

"I'm very pleased to meet you, Zuzu and you too, Pedro." She sat down, immensely relieved. "Can I ask what you're studying?"

"My brother and I hope to graduate with a law degree."

"In that case, today is my lucky day!" Beatrice beamed. "Let's order coffee and get down to business."

It took over an hour to explain her concept. The mayor listened impatiently while Zuzu or Pedro conveyed her message in Catalan for just over twenty minutes until his exasperation forced him to give up the pretence of not understanding English.

"This is crazy!" The excitement in his eyes belied his words. "It's not possible! Zuzu, is it possible? Talk to me, you're the lawyer."

"The answer is, it depends. If Señor Gallego already signed a contract, it's probably not possible. We would need to prove he signed under duress or was not in his right mind. The fact a security firm has already put markers around his land suggests has already transferred ownership. Pedro, what do you think?"

Pedro's gaze was distant. "I think it's possible that Suarez y Chan have overreached their authority, setting up barriers around the property they do not already own. Everything comes down to the contract, as Zuzu says. Let's look at worst case and best case scenarios. I'll go first, as the family pessimist." He gave them a lopsided grin. "Bertrand Gallego signed away his land rights to not only his home but the football field. The money is, or soon will be, in his bank account and the deal is done. Our only hope would be to challenge it on environmental grounds, on account of the well, or appeal to the regional government playing the social responsibility card. Neither of those options gives me much hope. In simple terms, the contract is between Suarez and Gallego, which means nothing at all to do with us. Zuzu?"

She mirrored her brother's grin and Beatrice had a flash of insight. These two were going to be a superlative legal firm. She could already envisage the advertising posters.

"Family optimist reporting for duty. Purely in practical terms, I question the timescale. Bertrand left here on Sunday morning. Today is Saturday. Suarez moves fast but no one could get a new contract drawn up, sent to the vendor, have it signed and returned in five working days. Let's be realistic, if she managed that, we could argue Bertrand had insufficient time to take legal advice on such a document."

The mayor's head switched from one to the other. "So yes or no?"

Pedro turned to look at Zuzu and for a second, Beatrice wondered the twins were capable of non-verbal communication.

"Let's prepare for both eventualities," said Zuzu. "Working on the assumption that Suarez has Bertrand's signature, Pedro can make a good case for a legal challenge due to emotional distress and undue pressure. Meanwhile, with Beatrice's help, I can talk to the inhabitants of Sirenes and explain our proposition. The presence and authority of the mayor would be influential."

The mayor chewed on his moustache. "I don't want to, you know, raise false hope."

"Nor do I," said Beatrice. "The trouble is that we do not have the luxury of time. If there's any way of gathering the villagers and explaining our idea this afternoon, I do believe that our only hope. Could you, as the mayor, call an emergency meeting?"

He looked at his watch. "Three o'clock?"

"Three o'clock would be ideal" said Beatrice. "Not only can we prepare ourselves, but we can also have a spot of lunch."

Not the fault of Hotel Salines, but Beatrice was far too tense and agitated to appreciate the food. Everyone else was occupied, either gathering the villagers, checking the financial situation, clarifying points of law or setting up seats in the community centre. Due to her lack of language abilities, Beatrice was useless, so sat at a table in the hotel, waiting for her phone to ring.

The waiter came to clear away her meal and asked if she would like a dessert. At that moment, her phone buzzed and she dismissed the young man with an apologetic smile.

"Mia! How did you get on?"

"*Bonjour*, Madame Stubbs. Bertrand Gallego *ici*."

Beatrice changed gear and put her brain into French. "Bertrand, *ça va*? Are you all right?"

There was a long pause before he responded. "Am I all right? Yes and no. I am in a car with Mia, Joan and Jesus, travelling to Sirenes. They tell me you have a plan."

"A plan? Yes, I have a plan. But everything depends on your contract with Suarez. If you have already sold your property, there's very little we can do."

She waited while he spoke to the others. "I signed nothing, Mrs Stubbs. The property still belongs to me. I have given my word that I will return the contract with my signature first thing next week. Señora Suarez will be expecting that document on Tuesday morning."

"Señora Suarez can wait a few days more, Bertrand. Will you allow me to organise an auction for your land? You can set a minimum price and anything over that is to your advantage. I will do everything in my power to make it happen tomorrow. Failing that, Monday at the latest. Do I have your permission?"

"Yes, you have my permission," he sighed. "You need to understand that El Castor and the Suarez woman hold all the cards. They can outbid anyone because they have the money to do so. I don't know what you're planning with such an auction, and I don't want to know because it will only end in disappointment for me. I'm returning this evening to pack up my home and leave Sirenes forever. I'm moving on."

Beatrice exhaled quietly. "That's your prerogative. I am grateful that you are prepared to open up public bidding. That's an honourable thing to do."

The mayor appeared in the hotel doorway, beckoning with both hands.

"I need to go now, Bertrand, I hope to see you over the next few days. Thank you for your trust and I wish you a safe drive home."

"I'm safe, Beatrice." He chuckled. "I'm in the hands of Jesus."

She laughed, more at the fact that she actually got a joke in French rather than the content of his words. Bertrand appeared to be on fighting form. That meant she had to throw everything in her arsenal at this afternoon's meeting. She paid the bill, gathered her things and hurried off to join the mayor.

"Much to talk about!" he said. "Teresa has information and we maybe need the police. Not everyone comes, very busy, but we have many people. Come, Zuzu and Pedro are already in place."

It wasn't so much that Beatrice expected a round of applause when she entered the town hall, but a sea of hostile faces and folded arms was an unnerving sight. She got straight down to business, hands on hips and wearing a ferocious scowl.

"Ladies and gentlemen, thank you for coming. The various arms of my investigation I outlined yesterday are still in progress, but I can tell you we have made a significant leap forward. Bertrand Gallego has agreed to put his property up for auction."

Most of the audience looked to one another for some kind of clarification. Beatrice waited until Pedro had finished his translation.

"This means that anyone can bid on Bertrand's land. My suggestion is that you, the villagers of Sirenes, come together and bid higher than everyone else."

Zuzu explained to a chorus of groans.

Beatrice hastened to add some context. "Wait a moment. You think you will be bidding against a huge enterprise such as El Castor. Maybe you will, maybe you won't. I am going to meet Juan Ferrara as soon as I can with the sole aim of persuading him not to buy this land. Whether I am successful or not remains to be seen."

A great deal of grumbling and shrugging animated the crowd after Pedro conveyed her message in Catalan.

Beatrice pressed on, determined to win these people over to her vision. "Even if I cannot keep El Castor out of the game, you can still win. Whatever they bid, you bid higher. You should bid more than you can possibly afford in order to snatch the sale. When that happens, you have up to ten days to withdraw your offer. What we're buying here, everyone, is time. If we can prevent the sale of Bertrand's property for another week, I believe we can prevent it permanently." She was speaking like an American politician, she knew that much, but somehow or other she had to rouse their passions.

A glance passed between Zuzu and Pedro. The girl got to her feet, visibly gathering her courage. To Beatrice's huge admiration, Zuzu echoed her tone, pointing her finger to the crowd, opening her arms and gesticulating with such emphasis that even if Beatrice couldn't have grasped a single word, she would have sworn allegiance to the message.

For the first time, heads nodded or swayed from side to side in acknowledgement of her point. They were warming to the idea.

Another voice spoke. Everyone turned to see the priest, Father Francis, standing in the doorway wearing his cassock. He walked through the crowd, his voice powerful and his tone impassioned. He held the villagers in thrall but Beatrice couldn't follow his rhetoric.

Zuzu whispered in her ear. "The father asks if they believe in *convivencia*, or living together in harmony. He does and so did Núria Soler. The people of Sirenes have a history of coming together when it matters, like after the freeze of '56 or the fire of '88. Some of us are too young to remember, but we have all heard the stories. The same principle applied during the COVID pandemic. Neighbour helped neighbour and we pulled together, rallying around those who suffered the most. We tell and retell these stories of courage and community spirit because we are proud of what we did. It means something to be a Sirenesenc. Our pride in ourselves and loyalty to each other is stronger than many other obligations. He will give us an example. Last night, he broke the law. Yes, he, a man of the cloth broke two commandments." Zuzu's eyes widened as she listened to the next sentence. "Under the cover of darkness, he and a compatriot entered the property belonging to our friend and neighbour Bertrand Gallego while the security guard was distracted. He took samples from the well. Why? Because it was the right thing to do. Saving this community is a thousand times more important than a police fine for trespassing on private property. Most of all, we owe it to Núria Soler. She cared for this village her whole life. We cannot allow her death to mean the death of our community. Because if Bertrand leaves Sirenes and big business takes over the football field, that is what will happen. We are sad, we are grieving but we are not defeated." Zuzu gave a little sob but kept going. "Sirenesencs never give up. *Convivencia* for ever!"

Applause broke out and the entire meeting got to its feet to give the priest a standing ovation. Beatrice noticed Raimon Soler at the back of the crowd, banging his palms above his head, his emotions barely under control.

Zuzu wiped away tears and Beatrice choked up. At a signal from the mayor, Pedro stood up and raised a hand for silence before he made his announcement.

"The mayor is willing to coordinate the village's bid," said Zuzu. "Whatever the community is willing to pay for the land, the council will match it." Beatrice glanced at the mayor for confirmation and he gave a single solemn nod.

The mayor slapped his hand on Father Francis's shoulder, stared at the villagers and pointed to his watch. Everyone scrambled to their feet and hurried out of the door. Beatrice glanced at Pedro.

"Everyone's going to the bank. This is actually happening. What next?"

"I think I need a lie-down," said Beatrice, taking a deep breath. "No, there's no time for that. We need to find an auctioneer and I know just the man."

15

The mayor loaned his car to Beatrice and the translation twins for the afternoon. Unexpectedly, Raimon asked if he could join them. Zuzu instructed Pedro to drive and Raimon to navigate, so she and Beatrice could sit in the back seat and prepare their arguments.

They drove out of the main square towards the motorway; the mayor, Father Francis and even Carlotta giving them the thumbs up from the doorway of the hotel. Zuzu used her tablet to show Beatrice everything she had found on Juan Ferrera. Head of Development at El Castor, a family man with three children, he had a fondness for golf and a head for languages. According to his LinkedIn profile, Ferrara spoke Catalan, Spanish, French, Italian, Arabic and English.

"I guess you don't need us after all," said Zuzu.

"I most certainly do," Beatrice disagreed. "All three of you. My concern is where would we find the man and how can we approach him without scaring him off?"

"It's Saturday afternoon," said Pedro, joining the motorway. "There's only one place he will be. His golf club in Sitges. Zuzu?"

She nodded and nibbled on a fingernail. "That's the obvious

place to start. I can't find a personal phone number, so if he's not playing golf, we have to try his house. That's a forty-minute drive away."

"We go to the golf club. Mrs Stubbs talks." Raimon's definitive statement brooked no argument.

Beatrice had seen the golf course during her stay in Sitges and wholeheartedly disapproved. It occupied a large chunk of land at the end of the beach and forced walkers to go the long way around instead of directly from the beach to the cliffs. Its manicured prissiness stuck out in stark contrast to the rugged coast. She cautioned herself against resentful feelings before even meeting Juan Ferrara.

"He's there!" said Zuzu. "I just logged onto the golf club's reservation system. He finished a round twenty minutes ago, so he's probably still in the club. I also found the most recent picture of his car. A black Porsche Carrera."

At least twenty percent of the vehicles in the golf club car park were black Porsche Carreras. Pedro parked near the exit and they walked over the sandy ground to the club, Beatrice leading the way. Some hostility from the staff was to be expected, as they were clearly neither golfers nor members. But as they came through the double doors, no barriers prevented their entrance, not even a person at reception. The four of them stood awkwardly in the foyer for a moment until Beatrice remembered this whole thing was her idea.

"Just wait there a moment," she said to the three young people and strode into the restaurant. She accosted the nearest waiter, gave him her name in peremptory English and claimed an appointment with Mr Juan Ferrera.

The waiter seemed unimpressed and jerked his chin at the bar. "He's over there."

A tall man in casual clothes with a jumper draped over his shoulders sat on a bar stool, leafing through a magazine. Before her courage deserted her, Beatrice marched up to him with a broad smile.

"Señor Ferrara? My name is Beatrice Stubbs. I apologise for introducing myself in English but I have it on good authority that you are something of a polyglot. Do you have a minute?"

He gave her a cool stare. "Are you a journalist?"

"Good gracious, most certainly not. I have a dim view of journalists after my time as a detective inspector with Scotland Yard. Did you have a good round of golf today?"

"A police detective?"

"Retired. The only detecting I do these days is which particular predator has been nibbling my lettuces. I'm sorry to interrupt, but I need to speak to you as a matter of urgency. May I?" She sat on the stool next to him without waiting for his permission.

"Your name, again? I missed it." He folded his magazine and crossed his legs.

"Stubbs. Beatrice Stubbs. Can I buy you a drink? The wines of this region have proved an education over the last two weeks, but I'm willing to learn more. I am a sincere fan of Penedès, Corpinnat and a cheeky little white I found in the supermarket that I can't pronounce. What would you recommend as a relaxing red?"

"I'm sorry to be impolite, but I have no idea who you are or what you want. Saturday is my day off. I don't network, talk shop or advise complete strangers on wine choices. Excuse me." He stood up and gave her a brisk nod.

"The Sirenes project is a poisoned chalice," Beatrice gabbled. "I mean that quite literally, Mr Ferrara. I'm here to tell you the land acquisition is subject to a police investigation. Tomorrow, the property will go to auction. You should advise your agent not to bid, unless you are ready for a protracted legal battle and a reputational stain against you and El Castor. Next week, evidence will be presented to the Vilanova i la Geltrú police department which shows the vendor is selling under duress. Find another site, that's my recommendation."

Ferrara snapped his fingers and a barman appeared. "Two glasses of Priorat." He sat down and met Beatrice's gaze. "This is my recommendation. You were saying?"

"And three sparkling waters for my friends," Beatrice added, leaning backwards to beckon Zuzu, Pedro and Raimon.

They started in English, out of politeness, but Raimon cracked first. The three teenagers presented an emotional, forceful case for why El Castor should have nothing to do with the Sirenes acquisition. Beatrice sipped her wine and watched Ferrara's responses, but he gave little away.

When Pedro summed up the situation in Catalan, he enumerated the reasons by counting the fingers of his left hand.

Ferrara stood up and gave a short bow. "I have listened to your arguments, all very well put, and I hear your concerns. I'll take this under consideration and talk to my lawyer. Enjoy what's left of the weekend. Goodbye."

He marched out of the room, stopping only to whisper into the ear of a waitress. Beatrice was quite sure he was instructing the poor girl to eject them immediately.

"We should go," she muttered and raised a hand to forestall the young woman. "We're leaving now. Please can I pay the bill?"

"Your drinks are on Señor Ferrara's tab, so no charge. Thank you and goodbye."

The trip to the golf club was the least conclusive event of the afternoon. In Sirenes, it was a different story. Bertrand had returned and ordered the security firm off his land. Amid great drama, posturing and shouting, they left, taking their tape with them. A podium and public seating was half built at one end of the football field in preparation for tomorrow's auction. Manu accepted Beatrice's plea to oversee proceedings and the mayor's team sent out an official invitation to all potential bidders. At this short notice, Beatrice couldn't imagine there would be many.

Beatrice was sitting in Hotel Salines with Mia and the mayor when a young woman walked in, her smile like a cat that got the cream.

"Teresa, *qué tal?*" asked the mayor.

"Good evening, everyone. I just returned from the police station in Vilanova. Bad news and good news. I'm afraid the water samples collected from the well are inconclusive. We cannot prove the well was contaminated. Then there is the glass. That is a different story." She checked over her shoulder to be sure no one was listening. "What our friends pulled out of the well is the base of a vodka bottle. The police have identified the brand and are draining the well for any other markers. On Monday morning, they will interview anyone with a motive for polluting Bertrand Gallego's source of drinking water. One of those will be Ona Suarez."

All four of them sat in silence, taking in the implications.

"I knew she'd done it!" said Beatrice, then checked herself. "But *she* didn't do it herself. That conniving monster hires people to do her shitty work. The police must examine her financial records and see who is on the payroll and ... yes, well, they know what to do. Congratulations, Teresa! You've given us our first breakthrough!"

Teresa's face lit up. "Thank you. It is worth it. Goodnight and see you all tomorrow."

They wished her the same and watched her leave.

"Poor thing must be exhausted," said Mia. "What a day! Bertrand is in his own home, Joan and Raimon can recover in their beds and we should get a decent night's sleep before tomorrow. Beatrice, would you like to stay here instead of returning to Vilanova? I'm sure we can arrange a room."

Beatrice was too tired to think of anything but her beautiful corner suite overlooking the Pasifaë sculpture. "No, thank you. The bus leaves in fifteen minutes and I intend to return to Vilanova. First thing in the morning, I will report for duty. Thank you both for your extreme efforts today. Sleep well and see you in the morning."

The mayor stood up and clasped her hand. "Thank you, Beatrice Stubbs. You are ... special."

She said her goodbyes and went to catch the bus. One of the young guns was behind the wheel so she dug out her purse to pay for her ticket.

The driver waved her away with a shake of his head.

She walked up the aisle to find a seat. Instead of sharp stares from her fellow passengers, everyone was smiling, nodding and clasping their hands as if she'd just scored a winning goal.

The effort of being modest sapped her remaining energy, so she returned every smile and went to sit on the back seat. Because tomorrow, anything could happen.

The first sign of optimism came sooner than expected. Her phone rang just as she was walking up the steps to her hotel.

"Adrian, hello! How was the trip home?"

"Hello, Beatrice. Oh, it was a breeze. Made it home in time to fetch Dolly from the dog-sitter and everything. What's going on with you?"

"One sec while I let myself in. I've just this minute come back from Sirenes. There, I'm back in my room. Lots going on, actually, but it looks like I'll be able to get my flight on Monday."

"I gathered something must be up. When I got home from

the gym this afternoon, I had three missed calls from Ona Suarez."

"Really? How did she get your number?"

"I gave her my card. As you said, I have nothing to hide. Anyway, she left increasingly urgent messages, asking if I was ready to commit to purchasing the land we viewed. She asked me to call her as soon as I got her message, but I thought I ought to speak to you first."

"How interesting!" Beatrice dumped her bag on a chair and sat on the bed. "She's obviously in a panic. You see, the land is going up for auction tomorrow and I fully expect her to bid high. Unless ... I wonder."

"You wonder what?"

"There is a chance El Castor has pulled out. I went to see Juan Ferrara today, appealed to his better nature. He didn't give much away and I thought I might have wasted my time. But if he decided to withdraw his offer, she needs to know she has another buyer. Hence calling you as a matter of urgency on a Saturday evening."

"Does Spain have auctions on a Sunday? I wouldn't have thought that was allowed in a Catholic country."

"Special circumstances. Manu is going to officiate for us. Will you call Suarez back and see what you can find out? Make absolutely no promises regarding the land, but say you're considering Sirenes and a completely different location in France or somewhere. Then let me know what she says."

"OK, I'll do that immediately. Will wants to know if you're staying out of trouble."

"Assure him I am on my best behaviour. Is it all right with you if I stay over on Monday night? My flight gets in rather late to travel down to Devon."

"Of course it's fine. I'll cook. Right, I need to make that call. Talk to you soon."

Beatrice poured herself a beer and sat on the balcony, watching the nightlife of Vilanova. Restaurants were filling up, music played from various bars, groups of people strolled along the promenade and a steady stream of traffic rolled along the beach road.

She thought about Juan Ferrara, his cool expression giving nothing away. Was it possible their intervention had taken effect so fast? The smell of chips wafted up from the street below and Beatrice's stomach reminded her how long it had been since lunch. She was just browsing the room service menu when her phone trilled into life.

"Adrian, did you manage to get through?"

"Yes. God, she's a horrible bully, that woman. Sweet talk, coercion, threats and then she practically yelled at me for refusing to commit."

"Did she say anything about the other buyer?"

"Not specifically. She told me there are lots of people desperate to acquire the land and I was making a big mistake by not grabbing my slice of the pie. In which case, why was she so furious with me? You know what I think? I'm her last hope. I have no proof but I'm an excellent judge of human nature."

"You're right. She's panicking. If she bids on that land without any guaranteed buyers, she's taking a massive gamble and could end up seriously out of pocket. Oh, I am so looking forward to tomorrow!"

"I almost wish I could be there, just to see her face. Will you let me know how it goes? I have to go now, Will's making lasagne. One last thing. Have you seen Clarence du Ciel again?"

"Who? Oh, you mean that chap in orange. No, 'fraid not. He's not easy to miss. But I'll keep my eyes peeled. Thank you, Adrian, you're very good. Enjoy your lasagne."

That settled it. She would have the vegetable gratin and a glass of red.

16

The village of Sirenes wore its heart on its sleeve. Just as the air of grief and despondency had affected Beatrice on her first visit, the electricity and excitement buzzing through the place on Sunday morning was tangible. While waiting for the bus from Vilanova, Beatrice was the only one at the stop. She imagined that was par for the course on Sundays. But shortly after she boarded, once again waved past by a different driver when she offered to pay, a stream of people in their Sunday best came chattering and smiling to fill the seats around her.

It was another day of sunshine and blue skies after the rain in the early hours. Freshly rinsed streets shone and the palm trees seemed brighter after the dust had washed away. The elegant arcs of the mermaids welcomed her as the bus cruised past and she had a sense of real fondness for this little village by the sea.

The square was crowded with people just out of church, all wearing smart clothes and bright colours. She spotted Mia in a cherry-red dress with a straw hat and patterned scarf, talking to a group of women.

"Beatrice!" she said, kissing her on both cheeks. "That necklace is a real eye-catcher. You look so stylish."

"Thank you. So do you, as always. Is there any news?"

Mia led her away towards the beach. "I'd suggest a coffee, but I'm already nervous. Yes, there's news. Some bad, some good. Bertrand didn't turn up for church this morning. That's unheard of. Father Francis had to change his sermon. It's a sign Bertrand has already left the village, if not physically, then emotionally. On the brighter side, we have only three acceptances from other potential bidders for the auction."

"That's good news? Weren't we hoping it was between us and the Suarez woman?"

"In real terms, it is between us and the Suarez woman. The other two who accepted are scavengers, hoping this won't make the reserve limit. Then they offer something well below the asking price for a quick sale. It often works when people need hard cash urgently. That's why it's important that Bertrand is not present in person. An agent must represent his interests so he cannot be pressured in the heat of the moment. Your auctioneer is just the person."

They sat on the sea wall in the shade of the church.

"Is Manu here already? I must go and say hello."

"He's down at the football field with the mayor. We invited him to join us for lunch after the auction is over. What a charming man!"

"He is, isn't he? Mia, who's going to bid on behalf of the village? The mayor?"

"Not the mayor. He could be seen as biased. Same with Father Francis. We took a vote this morning before church. The person bidding on behalf of the village is Joan Soler."

Beatrice shivered despite the warmth of the sun. "How perfectly apt." She watched seagulls swoop and squabble over something on the beach. "Were he and Raimon in church today?"

"Yes. Raimon was looking for you, in fact. He said he had a question. Shall we go and find them? You know, I wish I'd had my porridge this morning. Anything to quell these butterflies."

Beatrice got to her feet and they linked arms to walk back to the square. "Never a good idea to skip breakfast. I had a Spanish omelette and very tasty it was too. How come a Catalonian woman is a fan of porridge?"

"Two decades married to a Scot, that's how." She shielded her eyes with a hand, staring at a figure standing outside the hotel. "Is that who I think it is?"

Beatrice followed her sightline and spotted the tall black man in a petrol-coloured suit and top hat, as incongruous as a peacock in a hen house. "That's Clarence du Ciel!"

He turned at the sound of his name and broke into an open-mouthed grin. "Mia! With Beatrice! Why am I not surprised you two know each other? Good morning, ladies!" He gave a deep bow. "Is it too early for a Bloody Mary?"

They sat on the hotel terrace, drinking their Marys: two Bloody and one Virgin, and eating salty crisps. In his mesmerising voice, Clarence related the story of why he tracked Mia down after she had failed to turn up at his fashion show.

"Beatrice, this woman is one of my icons. I was watching her do photo shoots and killing catwalks before I could even spell my own name. She was an inspiration then and remains so to this day. Of course I'm going to invite her to my show. Then a VIP seat goes empty and I'm asking questions. Mia Macdonald, a no-show? Really? Why in the world would she do that to me? We're friends. We go waaaay back."

Mia reached for his hand and pressed it to her cheek. "Way

back. If I could have been there for one of my dearest friends, I would. Last week was a series of dramas and when things came to a head, the last thing I wanted to do was to rush off for a fashion show in Barcelona. I apologise. Was it a success?"

"Stratospheric, Mia. One of my best. *All* the usual suspects were in attendance, you were missed and we celebrated till the sun came up." He lifted his glass. "This is the hair of the hairiest dog and I'm damned if it's not working. Dish the dirt, my friend. I want to know how you two got together and what you're up to. If it's mischief, I'm in."

A Hyundai Tucson pulled up outside the hotel and Beatrice's subconscious sounded an alarm. "Oh shit!" she hissed. "That's Suarez! She knows me as Ms Quinn, assistant to a wine importer. I have to hide." She snatched up her bag and pushed back her chair.

"Take this," said Mia, taking off her hat. "An oldie but a goodie. No one will recognise you in a dramatic hat."

"Thank you." Beatrice scuttled inside just as the car doors opened. She made straight for the bathroom and didn't look back.

On Manu's advice, the auction was due to start at one o'clock. 'Hungry people get impatient and make rash bids. After lunch, people are slower, sleepy, less keen. One o'clock on a Sunday is the best time to build tension.' That made sense. Beatrice had made a legion of poor decisions on an empty stomach.

Mia's hat, her own sunglasses, statement jewellery and swishy trousers rendered Beatrice unrecognisable on the track to the football field. Not even Adrian, one of her oldest friends, would suspect ...

"Hello, Mrs Stubbs." Raimon peeled off from a pack of teenage boys pelting past her. The young men's feet thundered over the ground, kicking up dust like bolting mustangs yet every single one wished her a good day. Anonymous, she was not.

"Raimon, hello again. I'm not sure I thanked you for your support yesterday. It might be too early to say, but I think our words hit home with Señor Ferrara."

"Yes. He has called my house last night. He offers me a job next year." He checked his phone. "Apprentice? He wants that I am an apprentice."

Beatrice stopped and stared. "That is wonderful news. You must have impressed the man. Congratulations!"

The boy blushed, his dark brows shadowing his eyes. "Is an important day for us, no?" He mimed trembling hands. "For Bertrand, also." With a flash of a smile, he broke into a jog and caught up with his friends.

With a podium at one end and seating for around a hundred people, the football field seemed peculiarly foreshortened. Beatrice walked to the last row, head bowed and ignoring everyone. A young girl budged up to allow her the last seat.

Beatrice blew her a kiss, a gesture she rarely used, but the hat and shades bestowed a level of flamboyance she couldn't resist. She settled into her chair and surveyed the field.

On the podium at the end sat the mayor, Manu, Father Francis and the translation twins. She quashed the urge to run up there and say hello because she was supposed to remain inconspicuous. She scanned the crowd but no one resembled Ona Suarez. It was possible she had sent an agent to represent her. On the far left, she spotted Clarence's top hat, a flash of cherry red beside him. Before she could even debate the wisdom of moving, the mayor opened proceedings.

Unable to understand the verbal dynamics, Beatrice observed everything else, which told her plenty. The man who took charge of the event was dignified, impressive and as far from the weakened marathon runner Beatrice had met than she could have imagined. Manu wore a pin-striped suit, white shirt, sunglasses and an air of authority. He began his speech into the microphone only to be met with screeching feedback. He took a step away and sat down.

Two young men adjusted the amplifier and tested the microphone. Manu stood up to begin his speech again. A flash of movement out of the corner of her eye distracted Beatrice. The Hyundai parked at the gate and two men in dark suits jumped out. One of them opened the rear door and Ona Suarez made her entrance. A dusty-pink dress and matching jacket highlighted her tan and her figure, while her accessories, a black handbag, black heels, sunglasses and a dramatic black straw hat, warned people not to underestimate this woman.

Sandwiched between her bodyguards, she held up a hand to Manu and the mayor, an unmistakeable instruction to wait. Then she picked her way down the track. That was when the heels proved inadvisable. She stumbled once, twice and only avoided a fall by grabbing the arm of a henchman. Seeing as she'd held up the auction by drawing everyone's attention to herself, the crowd had little sympathy. Sniggers and mutters rippled from front to back until the woman who considered herself a VIP found a seat in the front row. Her assistants stood awkwardly beside the podium, clearly wishing they were less exposed.

From then on, things moved fast. Beatrice caught very little of the detail but sat entranced at the activity. Manu spoke at an exceptional speed, responded to invisible signals and repeated numbers over and over until someone reacted. The amounts bid flashed onto an electronic screen behind his head. 800,000. 820,000. Bidders dropped out until only two people remained in the game. One was Ona Suarez. The other, Joan Soler. Heads snapped between the two, instantly looking for a reaction. The price crept closer to a million Euros. Beatrice sat on her hands, for fear of making an excitable gesture and inadvertently entering the fray.

All at once, the crowd drew a collective breath and not a single person moved other than Manu, whose gaze flicked between the last remaining bidders.

"*Uno. Dos. Tres.*" He smacked his palm on the table and held it towards Joan Soler. "*Felicitats, senor.*"

The crowd erupted into applause, leaping to their feet and cheering, hugging one another and laughing. Beatrice sat in her chair, teary-eyed at the spectacle. Emotions spilled over into boisterous air-punching and spontaneous kisses, until a shushing spread from the front. Beatrice stood up, but still unable to see above all the heads, she finally clambered onto the bench.

Joan Soler walked down the centre aisle, took a right and stopped in front of Ona Suarez. He held out a hand. Her two henchmen sprang into action, the first they'd seen all day, to flank their mark.

Suarez might be a cynic and a charlatan, but she could read a room. Or in this case, a football field. She stepped forward, shook Joan's hand and spoke into his ear. Then she held out an arm for one of the suits' support. The three of them made an uncomfortable exit, with all eyes on the incongruous trio until the Hyundai departed in a cloud of dust.

Released from politeness, the villagers celebrated with stamping feet, cupped clapping hands and riotous laughter. Beatrice joined in, unable to resist the infectious atmosphere. A little boy grabbed her hands for a dance, weeping women embraced her and kissed her on both cheeks, and so many hands patted her shoulders she felt like a spaniel.

17

"**B**ut where is Bertrand? This is his celebration more than anyone else's." Beatrice asked Mia as they walked back to the hotel. The mayor had invited everyone to a party, including relative strangers like herself, Manu and Clarence.

"He went for a hike in the mountains. I can't blame him. Few things must be as painful as watching your home being sold. The mayor sent a message with the good news so I hope he'll join us at some stage. Then again, it might be too emotional. Poor man, he's been through so much and it's not over yet."

"Selling one's property is an emotional moment. I've seen more tears shed over a parcel of land than any artwork," said Manu. "But if he agrees to the plan, he can stay, right?"

Mia waggled her head. "If he agrees. The man is the very definition of stubborn."

"Does he know what Teresa found in the well?" Beatrice asked, following Clarence up the hotel steps and taking a moment to admire his shoes.

"Oh yes, of course. But Bertrand, how can I put it? He's an

eternal pessimist. This is why he makes an excellent football coach and director of the *castellos*. He leaves nothing to chance, always convinced that the worst will happen. Last weekend, it did. As far as he's concerned, nothing will bring Núria back and he has to live with that for the rest of his life." Her tone contrasted with the vivacity of the dining room where chairs and tables had been pushed against the wall and a few men with acoustic guitars were tuning up on a corner podium.

"This is about as authentic as it gets. I love it," said Clarence with a broad beam. "What can I get you to drink, my friends? Under the circumstances, may I buy us a bottle of champagne?"

"Not champagne," said Beatrice. "Let's go local and have a Corpinnat."

Manu laughed. "Spoken like a true Catalan."

"Yes. We'll toast the villagers' success with a bottle of Corpinnat and could you order a large bottle of water?" asked Mia.

Clarence bowed and went to the bar. His style, normally a magnet for attention, seemed to attract little fuss, as if he had already been accepted as a friend of Sirenes.

"Sitting out in the middle of the football field at the hottest time of the day was a little too much," sighed Mia, wafting her hands around her face.

"And you had no hat because you loaned it to me! I'm so sorry. I feel rotten, especially as I needn't have bothered. Suarez had zero interest in the crowd. Have you caught the sun?"

"No need to apologise, it was my idea. Anyway, Clarence carries a parasol everywhere he goes so I was protected. Even so, I'm glad to get inside. Manu, you were so kind to come out here and officiate on a Sunday."

"When I heard the circumstances, I could not refuse. I feel lucky to be here."

Mia placed a hand on his arm. "Thank you. Are you pleased, Beatrice? After all, this was your doing and everyone is more grateful than we can express."

The room was filling up with happy faces. "None of us would be here if it wasn't for your dogged conviction Bertrand was innocent. I am pleased, in a vicarious sense, and will take a keen interest in the next stages. You will keep me informed, won't you?"

Clarence placed a champagne bucket on the table and poured four glasses. "I propose a toast to your success. It takes a special kind of grit to take on the establishment and win. Here's to you to, Rosemary and Thyme!"

Normally, Beatrice detested comparisons to fictional lady detectives but on this occasion, she could see his point. "Also to Manu's professionalism and your smash hit fashion show. To our successes!"

"To our successes," they chorused, over the increasing noise level of cheerful celebrations. The room was crowded and people spilled out into the rear garden or front terrace. The musicians struggled to make themselves heard over the din of conversation, but every time they finished a song with a flourish, they garnered a smattering of applause.

Mia was repeating a question regarding Beatrice's flight times the following day when the noise abated and people told one another to quieten down. The crowd made way for the mayor, his hand on the shoulder of Bertrand Gallego. The two men walked towards the musicians where the mayor commandeered the microphone.

He spoke in Catalan. Beatrice and Clarence exchanged a look of mutual sympathy at being excluded by their lack of linguistic ability, but Mia held up her index fingers to indicate she would translate soon as there was no risk of missing anything. It was the right decision, because not a single person in the room made a sound during his speech. Finally he paused and extended an arm to invite Joan Soler to stand beside him.

Mia hurriedly summarised what the mayor had said in English. "He congratulates the villagers on winning the auction against all other bidders. They are prepared to honour their commitment and buy the land, if that's what Bertrand wants. However, they have an alternative proposal. If he is willing to remain in Sirenes as football coach and *castello* director, they will withdraw their bid and the property remains in the owner-ship of Bertrand Gallego. The mayor and all of those who contributed to the bid have a suggestion. He's handing over to Joan Soler."

Joan must have been at the other end of the room because it took him a while to arrive at the microphone. When he did he held out a hand to Bertrand. The two men shook and Bertrand looked on the point of collapse. Joan spoke in clear short sentences, using all his rhetorical power. To Beatrice's surprise, once he had finished his brief speech, he switched to English.

"Now again in English, in recognition of how much our British investigator Beatrice Stubbs helped us. Bertrand Gallego is as much a part of Sirenes as the sea or the church. My son Raimon and I join with everyone else in entreating him to stay. Stay as our football coach. Stay as our *castello* director. Stay as our friend and neighbour. The one thing we would like to request is that we rename our football field from Camp de Futbol Sirenes to Camp de Futbol Núria Soler. What do you say, my friend?"

Mia clutched Beatrice's hand, biting her lip.

All eyes were on the stocky man in his walking boots. He pressed his hands to his eyes looked around the crowd, clasped his hands in prayer and swallowed.

"*Camp de Futbol Núria Soler sone bé. D'acord, em quedo.*"

Beatrice didn't need a translation because the reaction from the entire room was joyous. The mayor and Joan took turns to embrace Bertrand, kissing him firmly on both cheeks. People formed a disorderly queue to do the same, most with tears running down their faces. Even Clarence had pulled out a turquoise handkerchief to blow his nose.

"He's staying." Mia's face creased into happy tears. "He's staying in Sirenes."

The reaction when she relayed the news over speakerphone to Adrian and Will was not dissimilar.

"Oh my God! Will, did you hear that? That dear sweet man gets to stay in his family home, not ousted by some cynical corporate viper for a soulless supermarket. It's too beautiful. Pass me the kitchen roll. Beatrice, even Dolly's tail is wagging. This is better than 'Call the Midwife' and I only wish I could have been there."

Will's voice chimed in. "That dear sweet man who you never even met? The one who had to be, in your own words, 'out of his mind to want to live anywhere else than Cadaqués'? It's great news, Beatrice, and I feel personally touched that Manu officiated. Listen, I take back what I said about your extreme theories. I really hope the police do find evidence someone was messing around with the poor sod's drinking water. Good work, PI Stubbs."

"Thank you. It's even more of a tearjerker than you think. In two weeks, there is a festival in another town I can't pronounce. This Sirenes *castello* crew are going there to take part in the human towers. Bertrand Gallego will be right at its heart."

From Adrian she could hear only sniffs but Will spoke. "That is incredibly touching. It really does take a village, right? Are you coming home tomorrow?"

"Definitely. Mia and I are going into Barcelona tomorrow morning for a little shop and a ladies' lunch. Then a flight home and I should be with you by half six. What shall we do? Get fish and chips or go out for a pie?"

"No chips and no pie!" Adrian insisted. "It may have escaped your notice because of all the fun you're having, but we are attending a Paris fashion show on Saturday. Will and I have fabulous outfits, inspired by you, ironically. No carbs, no wine and daily workouts."

"Yawn. What a fuss. Catinca's show will last less than half an hour. You're dieting for two weeks, denying yourself all pleasures just to sit on the bench for thirty minutes when everybody's going to be looking at the models. Will? Talk some sense into him."

"You know what he's like. I can't ..."

Adrian interrupted. "When did you speak to Catinca? I've had no response to any of my messages for the last week. How come you have the hotline?"

Beatrice realised she had just put her foot in it. "Her people chased me because I hadn't confirmed and I asked how long this do would go on. Half an hour, they said. But we can get there early for some nibbles to show off our togs, I suppose. What's the news on the Netherlands?"

"We can discuss all that tomorrow," said Adrian, his voice testy. "Talking of togs, what exactly are you going to wear, Beatrice Stubbs?"

"Well, you see, that's exactly why Mia and I are going shopping. She has an excellent eye and all the right contacts. Ah, room service is here. I am going to eat my last paella on the balcony and watch the moon rise. See you tomorrow, chaps."

She closed her laptop, picked up her cashmere wrap and handbag then left the room. On her last night in Catalonia, it seemed a waste to dine alone. She went downstairs and out onto the street, looking for somewhere lively with the view of the beach.

18

Security outside the venue was tight. The doormen scrutinised her ticket and allowed her to enter with the kind of snootiness only Parisians can manage. Beatrice had to show her invitation on three different occasions. The third time was to enter the backstage area where the pre and post party would be held. She was early, unfashionably so, but Beatrice didn't care. She was bursting with excitement to see Catinca, never mind all the celebs.

Once permitted to enter the green room, Beatrice was disappointed. She expected wall-to-wall glamour, not a tatty dressing area which looked like a particularly disorganised laundry. A herd of lovely young women milled about, talking into their phones, touching up their make-up or submitting to the ministrations of one of the hairdressers. No one even noticed Beatrice and she began to wish she'd waited and arrived with the others.

After a minute, a child of around twelve, dressed in a shirt with a Mandarin collar, came over with a clipboard.

"Hello, you must be Beatrice. Catinca said you'd be early. I'm Van, one of her team on the ground. I know, makes me sound like I work at an airport." He or she rolled kohl-rimmed eyes.

"Let's go find the woman of the hour, shall we? Coffee, juice, glass of bubbles?"

"Bubbles, please." She was trying to think of a polite way of asking this person their age when she spotted Catinca scowling at a laptop.

"Cats, your guest of honour is here!" trilled Van. "I'll see to those bubbles for you."

Catinca whirled around and burst into a huge grin.

"Beatrice! You came! I thought you was gonna do your usual and duck out in favour of a case. Gimme a hug."

The two women embraced tightly.

"I'm sorry to barge in before you're ready. I just wanted to see you before the mayhem started and say thanks for wangling me another invitation."

"You *are* kidding, right? You're bringing Clarence du Ciel to one of my sodding shows! The gratitude is all mine, mate. You look fab, by the way. I recognise the dress, but that jacket is to die for. Don't tell me that's one of his?"

"No," said Beatrice, "it's vintage Givenchy. On loan from Mia."

"You're a jammy cow, you are. It looks fantastic on you. Where is your new BF?"

"She took Adrian and Will on an insider's tour of the city to walk off our lunch. Clarence is making his own way."

"Ha! First name terms!" She looked over Beatrice's shoulder where another youngster barely out of short trousers was signalling and pointing at his watch.

"Gotta do the walk-through. Come and watch with me. I want your opinion."

They walked through the glorified ladies' toilet and into the auditorium. In Catinca's company, no one requested proof that Beatrice was supposed to be there. The black-clad teen ushered them to a pair of cushions right at the end of the space.

Catinca and her aides talked in low voices about elements of the show in such technical detail, Beatrice lost interest.

Van appeared with a glass of champagne and a warm cheese puff. "Unusual combo, I know, but a match made in heaven. Enjoy."

The kid wasn't wrong. She nibbled at her snack, careful not to get greasy crumbs on her outfit and took in her surroundings. Tiers of wooden blocks padded with fake-fur cushions lined either side of a raised catwalk. Canvas flats behind the blocks depicted monochrome snow-dusted mountains, jagged against a blue sky. The audience lights dimmed and those on the catwalk brightened.

Everyone stopped talking and ambient music floated out of speakers, suggesting fresh air and uplifting scenery. One by one the girls pranced down the runway, smiling, laughing and half dancing, swishing their clothes like ballerinas. The spectacle was pleasing, like seeing a parade of university students cele-brate the end of exams. The only thing Beatrice was unsure about was the clothes themselves. Jeans, a frilly shirt, leather trousers, a dress apparently made out of dishcloths and almost all of them wore big clumpy boots, even the one with shorts cut so short the pockets poked out. The strangest combination, like wearing a greatcoat over a bikini. When the show was over, no one clapped and it all felt rather anti-climactic.

Catinca gave her assistants notes and sent them off to carry out her orders. She turned to Beatrice.

"OK, lady, what kind of vibe are you getting?"

"Fresh, I'd say. It's upbeat and energetic and perfect for the start of summer. Made me think of the last day of college."

"Good. Energy is the dynamic here. It's the autumn/winter collection, though, so my angle is the joy of outdoors. Guests are arriving, let's go."

They returned through the dressing-room which had now

been partitioned off, one section for the models, another for the guests. This was more like it. A dozen tall tables bearing canapés, bottles of champagne and glittery balloons gave a place a party atmosphere.

Catinca pointed at the ceiling, where swags of blue fabric reflected rainbows.

"Was supposed to be above the catwalk but I got My Little Pony wobbles. Glass of Pol Roger to calm my nerves?"

"Yes, of course. Umm, the joy of outdoors? Is that why they were all wearing big boots?"

Catinca stopped in the act of uncorking a bottle and burst into cackling laughter. "That was the walk-through, Beatrice. Models wear their own clothes but practise the moves. Those ain't my designs! Tell you what mate, you cheered me up already. Hey, there's Will and Adrian!"

The party was in full swing when Mia arrived with Clarence. Even though Beatrice had already recognised half a dozen faces from the TV or the newspapers, Clarence du Ciel was unmistakeably an A-lister, turning all heads. His outfit was relatively casual – a wing-tipped white shirt with black jeans and cowboy boots – but he had a presence that filled the room.

Catinca boggled her eyes at Beatrice until she realised she was supposed to make the introductions.

"Clarence, can I introduce you to ..."

"I know who you are," Clarence grinned, taking Catinca's hand in his. "The most exciting young designer in Europe. Thank you for inviting me to your show. It's a privilege to be here."

"Thank you for coming. I'm thrilled to meet you. You're one of the reasons I got into fashion," Catinca gushed.

Beatrice decided to leave them to it. She wandered over to

join Will, who was examining a canapé while Adrian chatted to some actor she half-recognised.

"You look natty," she observed. He wore a mid-blue suit over a white T-shirt, highlighting his Barcelona/Sitges tan.

"Thank you. Or rather thank my stylist. I must say the same goes for you. Although I don't think we're supposed to use the word 'natty'. Everyone else is saying things like 'you're killing it', or 'rock that rad look'. I feel a total fraud." He flicked his eyes in Adrian's direction. "Not that it bothers some people."

"He's a social butterfly," said Beatrice, looking fondly at Adrian. He too wore a suit but with shorts instead of trousers. With his legs, he could get away with it. "Who's that chap he's talking to? I've seen him on TV."

"Chris somebody, part of the Marvel cast." On seeing Beatrice's baffled expression, he added, "Superheroes?"

"Oh, them. Quick, top up my glass. Looks like things are about to kick off." Several of the black-clad lackeys were guiding people towards the auditorium entrance. Adrian broke off his chat and came to join them, kissing Beatrice on both cheeks.

"Look at you, a style icon! Talking of whom, when do I get my introduction?" He jerked a thumb over his shoulder, unaware that Clarence was standing right behind him.

"How about now? Clarence, these are two very dear friends of mine. Adrian is a wine expert and used to be Catinca's boss. This is Will, his husband, a police detective inspector with the Met. Will, Adrian this is Clarence du Ciel, who's huge in the rag trade."

The men barely had time to shake hands before they were politely but firmly escorted to their seats. An excitable buzz of chatter filled the room, dropping to a hush of whispers anytime someone famous entered. A Hollywood actress was sitting in the front row opposite, between an ageing rock star and an Australian politician. The actress was much smaller than she appeared on screen and the rock star far older. Adrian nudged her and she realised she was staring. Their party of five got their fair share of sideways looks, which Beatrice initially put down to Clarence, but she soon noted how many fashion editors came over to offer their respects to Mia. The ex-model greeted each one by name. When everyone had taken their places, the lights dimmed and the show began.

Even though Beatrice had seen the models rehearse their moves, she was unprepared for the colour and energy that burst onto the catwalk. Gone were the clumpy boots and dishrag dresses replaced by flames of yellow and scarlet, wafting around the svelte bodies as if they were on fire. Bright frocks, shirts and jackets, with soft green velvet trousers and pixie-like boots, this was an animated vision of autumnal woodland. Impossibly beautiful men and women gambolled and pranced up and down the length of the runway, their enthusiasm infectious. The music reached a peak and a hooded figure took her place at the top.

"The bride," whispered Adrian.

It was a good job he'd said so because while Beatrice knew the frock was obviously the centrepiece of the collection, it was the least traditional bridal gown she could imagine. The cloak was the pale orange of a winter sunrise at the top, growing brighter over the shoulders, deepening into golden brown all the way down to earth at the hem. The model sashayed to the end and unclasped the cloak, letting it fall at her feet. Inside was a striking black girl, barefoot and wearing a silk tea-dress the colour of melted milk chocolate. She twirled and the hem floated up around her thighs. The crowd applauded and whistled their approval. Her headdress was made of woven autumn leaves, threaded with gold and studded with precious stones.

She returned up the runway to a barrage of camera flashes and the entire cast poured from the wings, Catinca in the middle. She'd changed from her pink shirt-dress into a grass-green satin gown and let her hair fall loose. Her lips, painted ruby-red, were stretched in a huge grin. She took her bows, blew kisses, high-fived the bride and returned backstage.

"Wow!" said Will.

For once, his husband didn't pour scorn on his lack of eloquence but wholeheartedly agreed. "Wow, indeed. What a debut!"

"It was a stunning collection, wasn't it?" said Mia. "From concept to execution, every detail was exactly right. Her talent is thrilling."

"It is," Clarence nodded. "That gave me gooseflesh. I don't know whether to congratulate her or cry because that woman is going to give every fashion designer in the world a run for their money. Want to go pat her on the back?"

They mingled with the VIPs moving into the party room. One woman gestured for Beatrice to go first through the door.

"Thank you."

"My pleasure. Did you enjoy the show?"

"I thought it was fabulous," Beatrice answered honestly. "How about you?"

"So, so good. And the bridal gown, oh my!" She fanned herself with her ticket.

Beatrice read the name and noted the woman was the American editor of a glossy women's magazine. "Quite. It was as far from the typical wedding frock as it gets, but utterly gorgeous."

"Let me ask you something. What did you see as the meaning behind it?" She accepted two glasses of champagne from a waiter and handed one to Beatrice. "I have a theory but it's kinda out there."

"Thank you. The meaning of the show as a whole or the bridal dress?"

"Well, I guess the two are connected but I was asking about the wedding gown in particular."

Beatrice thought about it. "Other than expect the unexpected, I really couldn't say. What's your theory?"

The woman tilted her head to one side. "Don't laugh, but for me, the cloak represents the earth. Beneath it, the gown with in its simplicity and colour, celebrates the organism that keeps the earth healthy and aerated – the humble worm."

Beatrice's eyebrows rose of their own accord.

"See, I told you it was out there."

"That's why you're a fashion editor and I am not," Beatrice laughed. "Should we run it by Catinca and see what she says?"

"You actually know Catinca Radu? Wait, you were sitting on the front row with Mia MacDonald and Clarence du Ciel, right? Oh Jeez, did I just put my foot in it?"

"Not in the slightest. Your theory will tickle her pink. Come and say hello. You don't have to mention worms if you'd rather not." Beatrice made the introductions and saw Mia beckoning from across the room. She excused herself and joined her friend.

"What is it?"

"I just heard from the mayor. Ona Suarez has been arrested. He doesn't know yet what they're charging her with or if the indictment will be linked to more than the death of Núria Soler. But it seems that vile woman's actions have caught up with her at last."

"Oh, that is wonderful news!"

"The best! The inspector would like a word on Monday morning, if you're agreeable. I can give you more details en route. Our taxi to Gare de Lyon will be here in twenty minutes."

"I thought the train to Barcelona departs from Gare d'Austerlitz?"

"It does. But Gare de Lyon has a restaurant called Le Train Bleu, an iconic dining experience with classic French cuisine, Art Nouveau decor and historical patrons from Dalì to Chanel. An experience I will not permit you to miss. I booked a table for six people. From there, it's a ten-minute walk to Gare d'Austerliz across the Seine. We find our train; settle into our private compartment and tomorrow morning, we wake up on the Spanish border. You still want to come?"

"Wild horses couldn't stop me."

19

The rocking of the train as it rattled out of the French capital made Beatrice wonder if sleep was a realistic prospect, but once she got used to it, the motion became comforting, like the slight swing of a hammock in the breeze. Mia had booked a first-class cabin just for the two of them, so they would not be disturbed. It was an excellent idea, and after they shared a half bottle of Bordeaux as a nightcap, they took turns to visit the bathroom, wished each other a good night and settled into their respective couchettes.

The usual flicker of regret crossed her mind, as it always did when enjoying an experience Matthew would have loved. The whole day ticked all of his boxes. Well, perhaps not the fashion show, but dinner at Le Train Bleu and a sleeper train to the south of France would have been right up his boulevard. Beatrice released a sigh of pure contentment. What a perfect day.

A mismatched ensemble in some ways, the six individuals around the dinner table at Le Train Bleu chatted and laughed like old friends. The dinner was in celebration of Catinca's show, so she was the centre of attention. Mia and Clarence were fashion folk and had plenty to talk about. No one needed to worry about Adrian. He was at home in every milieu. The only one who might find the whole experience overwhelming was Will.

Beatrice's concerns were unfounded. He marvelled at the interior of the restaurant, craning his head to look up at the murals which stretched up to the ceiling, pointing at the moulding and chandeliers like an excited child.

"I owe you an apology," he said, with a rueful smile. "You were right about Suarez. I accused you of over-imaginative theories and I'm man enough to admit I was wrong."

"You were absolutely right to do so. The question you asked was crucial. How could she pollute his well and be sure Bertrand would collapse when forming part of the *castello*? The answer is that she couldn't. In fact, she probably never even intended that outcome. Her aim, I see now, was to discredit him as an alcoholic. The man who preaches abstinence is a secret drinker? Her plan was to make him slip up in public and incur public approbation. Ashamed of himself and isolated from his community, she would offer him absolution and a wad of cash. That it happened at such a juncture could never have been foreseen. But because it was a literal fall from grace, people asked questions. The credit for this really must go to Mia."

The woman heard her name and raised her glass to Beatrice. "We made a good team."

Another toast. Adrian chose the wines to accompany Mia's menu suggestions. Everyone was in their element. At one point, after a full-bodied glass of something French, Beatrice gazed around the table and could almost picture the bonds forming. She grinned and accepted the fact she was more than a little squiffy.

It had been a wonderful trip, she reflected, rocking in her bunk. All topped with the news of the hateful Suarez woman's arrest. She curled onto her side and imagined waking up on the

French-Spanish border. All augured well for tomorrow. For the first time in her life, she was looking forward to a football match.

"How do you do it?" asked Beatrice.

Mia had woken her just before eight, carrying two cups of vending machine coffee, so they could gaze out the windows Castle Foix and the stunning Pyrenees. On arrival at Latour de Carol, Beatrice sat in the bistro, minding their suitcases and tucking into a Croque Monsieur, while Mia hurried away to do 'some errands'. By the time the Barcelona train pulled in, she was back with half a dozen Sunday newspapers and a 'pique-nique'.

"It's not the first time I've travelled this route. The Barcelona train has no buffet and it's another four hours along the coast to Sirenes. I learned the hard way how to get decent food and I'm desperate to read the reactions to Catinca's show. There was only one paper in English, sorry."

"Ooh, it's in the papers already?" Beatrice hurried after her and they found an empty table in the second compartment. "The travelling savvy wasn't what I meant. How come we both slept on an overnight train, but you look fresh and stylish, while I resemble a day-old galette?"

"You don't look like anything of the sort. Rear-facing or forwards?"

"Forwards, please."

"Fine. Spread your jacket on the seat beside you and I'll open all the papers. That way, no one will join us. Don't forget to look at the view. This side of the Pyrenees and the coast route is enough to make you cry."

She was absolutely right. Gushing reviews of Catinca's visionary fashion event absorbed her attention for the first hour and she did her duty by oohing and aahing when Mia translated excerpts from the French and Spanish press. Then she dedicated herself to the ever-changing landscape. Like a banquet for the eyes, every few kilometres offered something pleasing, extraordinary or noteworthy. Beatrice made no attempt to capture the sights on her camera, knowing the results would disappoint.

Her phone vibrated frequently with messages from Adrian, Catinca, Will and Clarence which amused and delighted her. Just as she and Mia were finishing their picnic, the conductor announced their imminent arrival in Vilanova i la Geltrú. For old times' sake, Beatrice made a plea for the bus rather than a taxi. Mia stressed the urgency of getting to Sirenes by 15.00 but on seeing the figure of Carlotta smoking by her vehicle, capitulated and they paid their fares.

The bus was passing the mermaids sculpture when the bells rang three o'clock. Mia twitched and peered out of the window.

"No need to stress." Beatrice rested a hand on her arm. "We'll be there to support them. Relax and stop frowning. It plays hell with the forehead."

Sirenes was like a ghost town. Everyone was at the game. Mia took their cases into Hotel Salines and instructed the receptionist to put them in her room. Then they started at a trot across the square, broke into a run down the dusty track to the football field, energised by the sound of the crowd and raced each other to the entrance. Using their legs after hours sleeping or sitting on a train was a welcome release. Exhilarated, sweaty and gasping, they laughed and greeted those villagers whose eyes were not glued to the action.

Sirenes were playing Castelldefels, old rivals even though the most senior members on either team were only seventeen. Benches ringed the field, mostly populated by older supporters, while younger cheerleaders stood behind them, volubly reinforcing their support. The place was packed, even more so than the day of the auction and the atmosphere celebratory.

Zuzu appeared at her elbow before Beatrice and Mia had caught their breath. "Just in time. The mayor saved you a seat. Come this way."

The stage previously used as an auctioneer's podium was now redeployed as VIP seating behind one of the goals. Two rows of seats were partially covered by sun umbrellas printed with the name and logo of Hotel Salines. Between the mayor and Joan Soler two empty places remained. Zuzu led them up the steps and went to sit in the second row, next to her brother and Father Francis. Their greetings were drowned out by the roars when a player scored a goal. Beatrice took her seat and applauded with everyone else.

"Was that one of ours?" she asked the mayor.

"Yes. Our team plays in turquoise, the opposition in orange. One nil to Sirenes!" he beamed.

Any thoughts Beatrice had of a quiet afternoon like those spent in Upton St Nicholas watching cricket on the village green were soon dispelled. The game was fast and relentless. The teenagers kicked up dust, tackled one another, yelled for a pass and once in a while, scored a goal. Beatrice was exhausted just watching them. At half time, the score was two apiece. The Sirenes players drifted off the pitch to the right, where Bertrand Gallego and two other men were dispensing water bottles. Bertrand was too far away for Beatrice to see his face, but his gestures were animated as he spoke to the boys. He squeezed shoulders, clapped backs and high-fived different players, adding energy and enthusiasm to the hot and dirty squad. Two substitutes warmed up on the touchline, their shirts brighter and cleaner than those of their team mates.

"That is a very nice colour they're wearing. There are Swiss lakes of a similar hue. You know, it reminds me of the turquoise patina on the Pasifaë sculpture or the Sirenes mermaids."

Mia cocked her head and looked at the shirts as if for the first time. "How curious. I'd never thought of that. To me, it's closer to Fortnum and Mason's eau-de-nil or the classic Tiffany blue."

Beatrice chuckled. "You're a fashionista to your bones, aren't you?" She turned to Joan. "Is Raimon playing today?"

"Sure. He's in goal. He'll be down this end for the second half. What do you think of the dedication?" He indicated an enamel plaque propped up on a table. An intertwining border of turquoise and yellow framed the lettering.

CAMP DE FUTBOL NÚRIA SOLER
EN MEMÒRIA D'UNA GRAN DONA

"Oh, that is lovely! And to have it in the same style as the street signage makes it feel part of the town. Where do you plan to put it?"

Pedro answered. "At the entrance on the concrete gatepost. That way everyone will see it when they arrive."

"We had a minute's silence for Núria before the match, followed by a naming ceremony," added Zuzu.

"I'm sorry we missed that," said Beatrice. "My fault for insisting on the bus."

Joan shook his head. "It was something for the villagers. You arrived exactly at the right time. Ah, here we go."

The second half commenced at the same furious pace, although the temperature after the sun's zenith was mellower. Raimon saved a goal and Beatrice leapt to her feet with everyone else, banging her hands together until they hurt. A debate ensued after two attackers collided and the referee threatened to send the pair of them off unless they calmed down. Sirenes scored at the opposite end and the crowd became borderline delirious.

Beatrice checked her watch. Ten minutes to go. The Castelldefels coach switched three players in quick succession and the balance quickly changed. The orange team went on the offensive and made three goal attempts, only one of which Raimon was able to save. To Beatrice's great chagrin, the match ended with a clear win for the opposition. In her version of the story, Sirenes would have beaten their opponents five - nil and everyone lived happily ever after. The fact that most people seemed pleased with the result made no sense.

Mia said as much while they trudged up the same lane they had run down. "Don't get me wrong, I am happy the team can still play on their own field and under the guidance of Bertrand. I just wanted them to win."

A voice came from behind them. "They did win." Joan Soler caught up to walk between them. "Castelldefels teams nearly always thrash Sirenes and that goes for both senior and junior squads. They have more players, two coaches and plenty of resources. We are the underdogs. But we won't be pitied. If Castelldefels had gone easy on us today, it would have been an insult. They didn't. Everyone played a sporting game. In the last few weeks, we defended our field, regained our coach and today the under-18s played some scintillating football."

"Scintillating?" asked Mia, eyebrows raised.

"I sometimes watch Match of the Day. It improves my vocabulary. Are you staying in Sirenes this evening, ladies? Do you have plans for dinner?"

Beatrice liked Joan very much, but her craving for solitude had grown too loud to ignore.

"Unfortunately, I must decline. Tonight I return to my favourite hotel room in Vilanova. My appointment with the police inspector tomorrow morning requires detailed preparation. Then I head to Barcelona for a flight home. Mia's staying tonight, no?"

"Yes. But in a few hours' time, I will be walking down this track again. Bertrand has invited me to dine at his home." She lifted her sunglasses and her eyes sparkled almost as much as her earrings. "We have lots to catch up on."

"Hooray!" Beatrice hooted. "He is a lucky man. We must have a glass of fizz before I catch my bus. Joan, I would like to invite you to join us. Raimon too, when he's ready."

Joan put one arm around her shoulders and the other around Mia's. "It would be an honour."

It was getting dark by the time Beatrice said her emotional farewells, promising to come back as soon as she could manage it. She embraced the mayor, Joan, the twins, Father Francis, Bertrand, Raimon, Teresa and Mia at least three times. Her return was guaranteed as a matter of legal procedure because she would be a witness for the prosecution.

Joan heaved her case into the belly of the bus and thanked her once again.

"You saved Sirenes, Beatrice."

"Nonsense. As you well know, it takes a village. Goodnight, Joan."

She clambered onto the vehicle, Carlotta waved away her attempt at paying her fare and Beatrice found a seat on the right, best positioned for viewing the mermaids.

On an average evening, two spotlights lit the sculpture from below. Tonight, the moon, full and brilliant, bestowed its celestial shine from above. Sirenes, forever entwined, at once fixed and in motion, together for eternity.

MESSAGE FROM JJ MARSH

Dear Reader

Thank you for reading *Siren Song*. I hope you enjoyed Beatrice's adventures.

Have you met my new heroine yet? She's the main character the Run and Hide series and her name is Ann Sheldon. Or is it?

If you'd like a taste of what to expect, turn the page for the first chapter of *White Heron*.

If you would recommend this book to a friend, please do so by writing a review. Your tip helps other readers discover their next favourite read. Your review can be short and only takes a minute.

Thank you.

EXCERPT FROM WHITE HERON

My name is Ann Sheldon. A tourist? Yes, but having hopes to become a local. I'm a poet. I hunt peace and quiet and inspiration. Ha, ha! Very little money in poetry. No, not rich and not American. I come from a small village in Britain nobody knows. Oh, the wedding ring? My husband is dead several years. Thank you, that's very kind. I like very much to stay here, but I don't know how long. The plan is to survive the rainy season and take profit from the summer, but we'll see. So beautiful this island, you're lucky. I must return to my poems. Nice talking to you, have a good day.

Just fluent enough to be understood with sufficient mistakes to mark her as a *gringa*. It takes practice to do something you do well badly. Ann practised and did very badly indeed. Patronising looks, amused smiles and gentle corrections were proof that her strategy was convincing. The weather worked in her favour, keeping people mostly indoors, so that her occasional encounters were generally limited to a nod and a smile from beneath her umbrella.

Speaking the language poorly was only one of her achievements. In all her other skills, she aimed for excellence. Security took priority and she devoted several hours a day to ensuring her shack was as safe as she could make it. Not quite an underground panic room but there were ways of protecting herself, even in a wooden hut on a Brazilian beach.

The old woman who negotiated the six-month rental had made no secret of her bewilderment. "But there's nothing there," huffed Dona Emilia. "Just rain and mosquitoes and water buffaloes until the rainy season is over. The restaurants are closed, there is no market and even if you bring food from Soure, how do you want to cook? There's no electricity, no Wi-Fi, none of the things you people want. It's not a good place for a single lady, I'm telling you."

Ann stood her ground and due to the woman's own downselling of the place, managed to rent the house for a pittance. What she saved on accommodation, she spent on purchasing a generator. As the old lady had said, certain things she did want. Whether it was a good place for a single lady or not, Ann could think of worse. She spent two weeks fixing the place to her own specifications. For a driftwood shack with a corrugated tin roof on a remote beach, it was the equivalent of MI5.

Nothing here, Dona Emilia? Ann had never heard anything further from the truth. Cranes and blue herons clattered out of the jungle, often heralded by their plangent call, the sound of a grieving widow. Cormorants and vultures scanned the shoreline for fish corpses and snatched the odd unwary crab. Buffaloes lumbered in and out of the mangrove swamps, giving her no more regard than a snort. When the rains ceased for a moment, Ann wandered along the edge of the jungle, spotting hummingbirds, a group of foraging capybara and squirrel monkeys shrieking from the trees. She retreated to the safety of her hut. The monkeys were warning each other of a predator; perhaps an alligator or a leopard. She didn't stay to find out which.

Above her head, a hawk was trying to escape a pair of kiskadees dive-bombing it from above, releasing their two-syllable curses. This little corner of the world teemed with bird, animal and insect life. The only thing missing was humans. And that was exactly what made it perfect.

People were naturally curious about this foreigner coming to dwell amongst them in the most inhospitable months of the year, but after discovering her name and marital status, they generally left her alone. She limited herself to the minimum of pleasantries and discouraged small talk. Her nearest neighbours, around a kilometre up the beach, were a young couple who seemed to do nothing but argue. They showed no interest in her, for which she was grateful. The days passed peacefully enough as she tended her tomato plant on the veranda, sewed up tears in her clothes and made soup once a week. One evening, when the sun began to set, she buried broken bottles in the sand, jagged side up, all around the property except the path leading to the steps.

Depending on the severity of the nightmares, she woke early and performed her exercises. Weights and skipping, usually, or a beach run if the weather allowed. Twice she walked into Soure for provisions, which was a twenty-kilometre round trip. 20K was not unreasonable for her level of fitness, but half of it with a full backpack in torrential rain took its toll. She skipped the beach run the next day. She ate what the locals ate, not just out of a desire to blend in, but because she had no choice. Manioc flour, rice and cassava, black or red beans made up the bulk of her diet, complemented by plantains, papaya, tomatoes and açai. Fish was an occasional treat to begin with until she grew more confident about approaching the river fishermen returning with their hauls of crab, prawns and catfish. Buoyed by her success in negotiation, she tried her hand with the sea-going boats. Some days, she could score anchovy, tuna and *cação*; others, she was lucky to get enough scraps to flavour a stew.

The last few days she'd come back empty handed and her tinned or dried supplies were running dangerously low. Rain or no rain, she would have to buy something to eat. When the wet season ended, there would be a market, a bakery and even a restaurant at the other end of the beach. Fewer than two kilometres away. But when would the rains ever end?

One morning after a particularly horrible night of broken sleep, Ann was drinking coffee at the table, watching waves curl towards the shore while attempting to psychoanalyse last night's dreams. It wasn't difficult. In the most vivid, she'd been trying to carry an armful of live crabs over a narrow bridge. Whenever she dropped one, it fell into the water and vanished. People were watching for her from both riverbanks and every crab she lost meant more trouble. Her dream self yearned to release all the spiky, wriggling crustaceans into the river and dive in after them. Subtle, her subconscious was not.

Someone was walking along the beach in a sou'wester and a wide-brimmed hat to keep off the rain. Whoever it was carried a checked bag, the kind people use to take their clothes to the laundrette. The nearest laundrette must be three hours' journey away. When the figure took a right onto the wooden slats that passed for a path to her house, adrenalin shot through Ann's system. She slipped behind the front door, her hand resting on the machete, listening to her visitor draw closer. Footsteps thumped up the steps and the rap of knuckles on wood made her mouth dry and her pulse throb. Rehearsals were over. It was show time.

"*Olá?*" yelled a woman's voice over the constant drumming of the rain on the roof.

Ann opened the door to see the female half of the argumentative couple scowling over her shoulder at the rain. Her face cleared when she saw Ann.

"Oh, you are here. I thought the weather was too shitty to be out jogging, even for a crazy person like you. I'm Fátima and I've brought you something. Is that coffee I can smell? I'll leave my coat and hat out here or they will soak your floor. Come on then, I like mine thick enough to stand up a spoon."

Concentrating hard on comprehending the woman's fast, slangy Portuguese, Ann was too surprised to refuse her entry. "Hello, my name is Ann Sheldon. I come from a small village ..."

"Yeah, I know. I heard all about it from Patricio. You know he's overcharging you for the tuna, right? Don't let him get away with that. Next time, yell at him and call him a thieving son of a ... *ai, ai, ai*! What are you doing with that great big knife?"

Ann had forgotten she was still carrying the machete. "I was going to ... chop something. Doesn't matter." She closed the door and placed the knife behind the curtain. "Is black coffee OK? I don't have any milk."

"Black with plenty of sugar. What did you do to your arm?"

Ann looked at the cluster of angry red bumps on her elbow. "Mosquitoes. The candles don't seem to work."

Fátima's eyes followed her sightline and she picked up what was left of the citronella stub. She sniffed it and shook her head as if unimpressed. She wore a pink jersey with faded jeans, wet from the knees down. Her thick hair, plaited to one side of her head, was the same muddy putty colour as the river when it tumbled into the sea. Her age was difficult to pin down, but she could be no more than a couple of years younger than Ann. Twenty-nine, perhaps? With sharp eyes and a ready frown, her expression cleared when she saw the coffee cup on the table. She even lifted the corners of her wide mouth into a brief smile.

"Candles are a waste of time and money. Get yourself some *jambú* plant, they hate that. Or better still, a net. Nuno, that ugly little gnome, usually has a couple to sell in among his fishing gear. Tell him I sent you and you can also tell him that if he tries to charge you any more than 20 reais I will kick his dirty arse. This coffee's not bad. Don't you have any aguardente? Or whisky, brandy, anything to give it something extra?"

"Umm, yes, I think I do have some whisky somewhere." Ann rummaged through her dry goods cupboard and found a half bottle of Tullamore Dew she'd bought on impulse at Duty Free. She tipped a slug into Fátima's cup.

With an approving nod, her guest grasped the cup with both hands and took a sip. "Now that's what I call a good morning coffee. After this, I can face the walk home. Don't you want to know what I brought you?" Fátima threw a glance at the bag.

"Oh, yes. That's very nice of you."

"Wait till you see what it is. Are you squeamish?"

Ann didn't recognise the Portuguese word. "Am I ...?"

"You know, delicate." She mimed covering her eyes and fainting.

"No, I'm not." Her voice sounded convincing but she eyed the bag with some trepidation.

Fátima leaned over and hauled out two dead chickens by the feet. "Fresh. Killed them myself before bringing them over here, because you don't look like the type who can wring a chicken's neck. That idiot brought half a dozen live ones home from Soure, then tells me he's off to Belém for a week. What am I going to do with six bloody chickens, I asked him? Keep them till you're ready for a chicken stew, he said. Keep them where? In my bedroom? His brother must be using the family brain cell this week. Anyway, I cooked two, exchanged a pair for a bag of potatoes and thought maybe you could use a couple. You eat so much fish, you'll start growing scales."

The dead birds lay on the table, scrawny and bedraggled and completely unappetising. Ann remembered her manners. "What a kind thought. I must give you something in exchange, as a good neighbour. I haven't been to the store for a while, but …"

"I don't want any food. Next time you see a bottle of whisky, think of me. What happened to your husband?" Her gaze rested on Ann's left hand.

"He died."

"Yeah, I heard that. How did he die?"

She told the truth, for a change. "He had an accident at work. What does your boyfriend do? Or is he your husband?"

The woman snorted, threw back the rest of her coffee and got to her feet. "As if I'd marry anything that stupid! I'd rather marry one of these." She prodded the limp poultry. "He works for the ferry company. At least until they realise what a workshy bone-headed lump he is. Before I go, I have another question for you."

Ann's heart sank. "What's that?"

"I want to know why you're so scared. Don't look surprised, I've seen you. Sticking broken glass around this hut, the bolts on the door, that crazy big knife, you're as jumpy as a squirrel monkey. Is someone after you? Tell me, what are you frightened of?"

Five minutes this woman had been in Ann's house and she instantly hit the target. *This is why you should never talk to people.*

Ann unclenched her jaw with an effort, but lied with more ease. "Everything. I travelled here from Rio de Janeiro and learned to be security conscious. I was robbed three times."

"This place is nothing like Rio! For a start, Rio de Janeiro has some decent men. You don't need to be scared of us. Unless you're afraid someone is following you?"

Her eyes narrowed and Ann faked a laugh.

"Who'd be following a poet?"

"If that's what you are. Anyway, I'm going now. Enjoy the chickens. Hey, the *padaria* opens tomorrow morning. Finally the village comes back to life. The rains have lasted for ever this year in this shitty place. As for you, poet lady, leaving Rio for this godforsaken backwater? You need your head examined. *Tchau*."

She muttered to herself while hauling on her raincoat and hat, then with a wave, or perhaps a wag of her finger, she splashed off down the path towards the beach. Ann watched her go and turned to face the chickens. Where the hell did she start?

Three hours later, she finished cleaning the house. It wasn't just the feathers and mess she'd made while preparing her chicken stew, but erasing all evidence of her visitor seemed almost more important. She didn't want anyone in this house. Next time anyone came to the door, Ann would talk to them on the veranda. As it was, Fátima's knowledge of her circumstances showed that the *gringa* was a subject of local gossip. Now everyone would know the foreigner carried a big knife, drank whisky and had a bad reaction to mosquito bites.

She stirred the pot, half resentful and half grateful to her intrusive neighbour. This would be the richest meal she'd enjoyed for months, despite the limited amount of flesh on the fowl. She sighed. Even when selecting her destination, she knew there was a greater chance of remaining anonymous and out of sight in a big city. Greater chances too of someone catching up with her. The list of pros and cons was extensive, but overall, a remote fishing village in North Eastern Brazil came out top. As for nosy neighbours, she reiterated her promise. *Just keep yourself to yourself.* She tested the meat, bit into a potato and pronounced it done. This would last her a couple days and then she could make a stock with the bones. Look at her, making the most of the local produce. Next she'd be shimmying up palm trees to lop down a coconut for breakfast.

She ate a bowl of stew while watching the curtains of rain glisten and billow in the moonlight. Maybe Fátima was right. She did need her head examined.

For Daniele and Guillermo, for giving me ideas

ACKNOWLEDGMENTS

With grateful thanks to JD Lewis, JD Smith Design and the citizens of Vilanova I la Geltrù

ALSO BY JJ MARSH

More in the Beatrice Stubbs European crime series

(Tap title to buy)

BEHIND CLOSED DOORS

RAW MATERIAL

TREAD SOFTLY

COLD PRESSED

HUMAN RITES

BAD APPLES

SNOW ANGEL

HONEY TRAP

BLACK WIDOW

WHITE NIGHT

THE WOMAN IN THE FRAME

ALL SOULS' DAY

TRUE COLOURS

≈

The Run and Hide series (International thrillers)

WHITE HERON

BLACK RIVER

GOLD DRAGON

PEARL MOON

My standalone novels

AN EMPTY VESSEL

ODD NUMBERS

WOLF TONES

And a short-story collection

APPEARANCES GREETING A POINT OF VIEW

For occasional updates, news, deals and a FREE exclusive novella, tap the link to subscribe to my free newsletter www.jjmarshauthor.com

Made in the USA
Monee, IL
31 July 2023

40243374R00114